WATSON

WATSON

A CAT IN A ZOMBIE APOCALYPSE

MAURO CROCHE

ILUSTRATIONS:
MARTY ROCHA

© Mauro Croche
Buenos Aires, Argentina

Instagram: @maurocroche
www.maurocroche.com

Dirección general: Mauro Croche
Diseño de Tapa e Ilustraciones: Marty Rocha
Diseño de interior y maquetación: Darío Delos

Table of Contents

1. A Hard Days Night...... 9
2. Homeless...... 15
3. The Wrong Human...... 21
4. Rex The Dog...... 27
5. The History of Kit-Ten...... 31
6. Fishing Day...... 35
7. The Red Eyed Monster...... 41
8. The Kit-Teen Bath...... 45
9. Zoo...... 49
10. Encounter With a Gorilla...... 53
11. About Cats' Ability to See Ghosts and Other Abilities   59
12. Watson Investigates...... 65
13. The Turtle...... 71
14. Rescue Plan...... 77
15. Nostalgies...... 81
16. Aliens...... 87
17. "I Want to See the World Burn!"...... 93
18. Escape Into the Darkness...... 97
19. Survivor...... 103
20. Puppy...... 107
21. Rex Talks on The Phone...... 113
22. The Last Can...... 119
23. The Attack...... 125
24. The Monster Returns...... 131
25. The Goddess of All Cats...... 137
26. Towards The End of The World...... 143
27. Author's Note and Dedication...... 149

CHAPTER 1

A HARD DAYS NIGHT

My name is Watson, and I'm a stray cat in the middle of a zombie apocalypse.

I wasn't always a stray. Once, I had an elderly human who fed me, sheltered me, and gave me a life of quiet contentment. With him, I was happy.

My human spent most of his time reading books about a detective named Sherlock Holmes and his loyal assistant, Dr. Watson. That's where my name came from.

The zombie invasion began in early spring, shattering our peaceful existence.

And for a cat like me, there's nothing worse than having your routine torn apart.

If we could, we'd live the same day over and over—gladly. Surprises and shocks are things we cats hate with all our hearts.

The zombie thing? That was a terrible surprise.

It caught us so off guard that my human—who never watched the news—turned on the TV, searching for answers. Normally, he only watched old science fiction and mystery films, but now the news became his world.

Day after day, we watched the horror unfold: people killing each other, biting, stabbing, shooting. The outbreak spread like fire, and soon it reached our town. From there, it didn't take long to reach the houses around us.

The first dead arrived on a full moon night. Three or four of them stumbled toward the house, and my human—his old hunting rifle in hand—took them down one by one.

The gunshots startled me, and I hid under the armchair, my heart pounding.

He kept firing. One shot. Another. And another. Seven bodies fell. I saw his hands tremble as he reloaded, but his aim stayed true. Not a single shot missed.

Then, silence. The moon drifted past the roof and disappeared behind the trees. My human, worn out and aged by the years, fell asleep in his chair. But I kept watch.

I patrolled the house all night, pacing through the rooms, peeking through the windows, and climbing onto the roof to keep an eye on the shadows below.

When dawn broke and I thought the worst had passed, I saw something in the distance that made the fur on my back rise.

A sea of zombies—dozens, hundreds—emerged from the forest.

They came in waves: men, women, and children, their mouths emitting an awful nasal wail, a grating "wuaaaa" that sent a chill down my spine.

I meowed in terror, waking my human. He took his position by the window and began firing again.

The gunfire was deafening, the air thick with smoke. I ran back to my hiding spot under the armchair, trembling. Shot after shot rang out, but through the large windows, I saw the dead growing closer.

First, they reached the stone path.
Then, they crossed the wooden fence.
Finally, they climbed onto the front porch.
And then—Crash! The windows shattered.
The dead poured in.

They threw themselves at my human and tore him apart. I watched, helpless, from beneath the armchair as they overwhelmed him. Even in his final moments, my beloved Food Provider searched for me with his eyes.

His trembling hand reached out toward me. His voice, faint and fleeting, whispered:

"Take care, Watson…"

And then, beneath a swarm of cold, dead hands, he was gone.

In that moment, something broke inside me. I knew my life had changed forever.

CHAPTER 2

HOMELESS

For several days, I wandered aimlessly around the house, lost, unsure of what to do or how to feed myself.

My human always provided for me—canned fish-flavored food or crunchy pellets from a bag. But now, the canned food was trapped inside the fridge, and no matter how hard I tried, that damned door refused to budge. As for the bag of dry food, it was tightly sealed, the plastic too thick for my teeth to tear through.

Two or three days passed, and hunger gnawed at my insides. I drank from the dripping faucet in the bathroom to quench my thirst, but soon even that small comfort disappeared when the water stopped flowing.

And then, the stench began.

My human—my beloved human—lay cold and broken in the living room. The dead had taken everything from him: his mind, his flesh, even his eyes. On the third day, the smell was unbearable, a heavy fog of rot that clung to the walls. A horrible thought crossed my mind—brief but persistent. I could… eat him. Just a little, just enough to survive.

The idea repulsed me. I shook it off, horrified at myself. To avoid temptation, I knew I had to leave.

So I said my silent goodbye and walked out the front door for the last time.

I needed to find a new human. I was too accustomed to comfort, too ignorant of how to survive on my own.

For days, I wandered through empty fields and abandoned farms, climbing trees at night to escape the wandering dead. The world had become a wasteland, scorched and lifeless. Farmhouses stood silent, their windows like hollow eyes, staring out at the dead bodies scattered across the land.

Some bodies remained lifeless, as they should have. Others—without rhyme or reason—rose again and stumbled aimlessly. I didn't understand why some came back while others didn't.

One thing was clear: the walking dead didn't care about me. They only attacked humans, as if drawn by something in their scent or soul. I was invisible to them—a ghost among ghosts.

It was both a curse and a blessing.

I moved cautiously, always listening, always watching. The disease had spread faster than anyone could have imagined. Survivors were scarce, fleeing in noisy cars or on motorcycles, their engines like growls in the silence. Food became harder to find. Every scrap was quickly snatched up by other desperate creatures—humans and animals alike.

One day, I reached a big city. My stomach growled with hunger. The streets felt heavy with loss, their once-bustling life replaced by shadows and silence. I missed my home more than ever—those nights by the fire, my human lost in his books while I dozed at his feet, safe and warm. Back then, fear was a stranger, and my belly was always full.

How much had changed.

Now I was thin, my ribs pressing against my fur, sleep a fleeting luxury.

I rummaged through an old trash can, hoping for something—anything—to fill the void. That's when I saw it. A large shadow moved toward me. I sprang toward a wall, my heart pounding, but the shadow was faster.

A hand grabbed my tail and yanked me down. I hit the ground hard, dazed and gasping for air. I blinked up at my attacker— a human.

But not a sick one.

This one was alive, healthy. His eyes gleamed with cruel intentions.

Before I could escape, he raised his hand and struck me. Once. Twice. Pain exploded through my body. The world spun, dark and disorienting.

And for the first time since the apocalypse began, I wished I had stayed hidden under that armchair, no matter how bad the stench had become.

CHAPTER 3

THE WRONG HUMAN

I think I passed out for a while. When I came to, I was no longer in the alley by the trash can, but in an empty lot. The human was squatting, his back to me. He had lit a fire and was warming his hands by it.

Taking advantage of his distraction, I tried to escape, but I realized my paws were tied. I began to meow in terror. The human turned to look at me.

—Ah, hello, kitty —he said, showing yellowish, crooked teeth that looked like a pig's—. I was just thinking about you. You're so beautiful! I love your fur. I think I'll keep it. I'll skin you and keep your pelt. But don't worry, I'll kill you first, I won't make you suffer. The rest of your meat will go into the fire.

He licked his lips as he said this. That's when I realized the human planned to eat me. I never imagined a human would want to eat a cat! Things must have been really bad for someone to do something like that. I writhed and tried to chew through the ropes, but it was useless.

Meanwhile, the human had taken a knife from his pocket and was approaching. His smell was truly awful—I had never met a human who smelled so bad. He placed his hand on my head, and I bit him. The man jerked back, cursing, and looked at his finger: it was bleeding. He looked at me again with wild, twisted eyes.

—You shouldn't have done that, kitty. Now I will make you suffer. First, I'll cut off your tail. And then...

A shadow rushed in at full speed. The human turned around, but it was too late: a monstrous dog, bigger than any I'd ever seen, slammed into him and sent him rolling across the ground. The man's knife flew from his hand and landed among the weeds.

The monster-dog lunged again, making the man scream in terror. That dog was truly savage! The human seemed to realize the same thing because he turned and fled into the night.

The dog turned toward me. His eyes were yellow and gleamed in the dark. Desperate, I tried to drag myself away. I was convinced this was the end, that the dog would devour me in one bite.

To make matters worse, I suddenly remembered a Sherlock Holmes book: *The Hound of the Baskervilles.* In it, a monstrous dog straight from hell attacked people and killed them mercilessly. I'd had countless nightmares about that damned story.

Now, it seemed, the hound had become real, and it was even more terrifying than in the book.

The dog came closer and rested his huge snout on my back. He started chewing on me. I meowed in terror and tried to claw at him, but my paws were tangled in the ropes. My back was arched so high I was surprised it didn't snap. My hind legs scratched uselessly at the dog's belly, but they didn't even hurt him.

—Hold still! —the dog suddenly said, and his words were so surprising that I froze—. If you don't stop moving, I won't be able to cut your bindings!

Stunned, I looked over my shoulder. I saw that, indeed, the dog wasn't eating me alive—he was trying to break the rope that held me!

After a few more attempts and a couple of fierce bites, he bit through the rope, and I was free.

I didn't waste a second and bolted. I ran like crazy, thinking this had been the most unbelievable night of my life.

I was already turning the corner, my paws slipping on the wet asphalt, when I heard the dog's bark—both curious and desperate:

—Hey, wait! Please! I need your help!

CHAPTER 4

REX THE DOG

His words made me stop. It was the first time a dog had asked for my help. Until then, every time a dog had spoken to me, it was either to insult me or to mock me.

Still keeping a cautious distance, I asked what kind of help he needed.

The dog, with brown and white fur, large ears, and a head the size of a wild boar, approached a pile of rocks and pulled out a kitten that looked at us with big, watery eyes.

—His name is Kit-Ten —the dog announced and gave him a huge, slobbery lick—. I have no idea how to take care of him, but maybe you do.

—And what makes you think I can take care of a kitten?

—Well… because you're a cat —he said, tilting his head as he looked at me—. Aren't you?

—Yeah, but…

—Wait, before you answer, I'd like to introduce myself. My name is Rex, and I'm a Saint Bernard. What's your name?

—My name's Watson, and I'm… a stray cat. Thanks for rescuing me from that guy, Rex.

—You're welcome, Watson. Where are your owners?

—Owners? —I let out a sarcastic laugh—. Cats don't have owners. Cats are free and wild. But if you mean my human… the zombies ate him.

—Oh, I'm sorry. My owner managed to escape before they got him. He's waiting for me now… in a place where all the humans are safe.

That made my ears perk up. I stepped forward to hear him more clearly.

—Wait, what did you say?

—That my owner is waiting for me in a shelter where the owners are safe.

—How do you know there's a shelter for uninfected humans?

—I heard it from my own owner.

—And your human is there? —I asked, suspicious—. Did he just leave you behind or something?

The big guy suddenly looked uncomfortable.

—Well… he had to leave quickly. There was a party happening.

—A party? Where?

—At my owner's house. And that's when the zombies showed up. They caused a big mess. My owner jumped into the truck and… —he looked at me, embarrassed—. In the confusion, he must have forgotten about me.

—And where did you even find that kitten?

—Oh, well, that's a sad story… —The dog licked his snout, as if recalling something painful, and began to tell Kit-Ten's story…

CHAPTER 5

THE HISTORY OF KIT-TEN

—I used to live on a farm —Rex began—. There were lots of animals there. I helped herd the sheep and cows with my master. I'm a herding dog, after all.

—Like a mastiff? —I asked, remembering the breed of the dreaded Hound of the Baskervilles.

—I think so... but I'm a Saint Bernard. Anyway, on that farm, there were also ducks, pigs... and a cat. Her name was Sizzy. We never really got along, and I think it was partly my fault because I always wanted to play, and Sizzy got annoyed.

—Mmm, yeah, I get it. Dogs can be really annoying. You don't understand that we cats need our privacy.

—She had kittens a month ago —the Saint Bernard continued—. There were six of them, each one cuter than the last. On the night of the zombie invasion, during that party, my master left and never came back. We were left alone—all of us. The ducks, the pigs, and my master's sheep. I tried to organize the farm, but the animals were so scared, and it was hard. A few hours later, the zombies came back. Only this time, they weren't humans... they were pigs.

—Pigs?

—Yeah, at least fifteen or twenty wild pigs, all of them infected. I tried to stop them, but there were too many, way too many. They killed everyone... the ducks, the rabbits, and my master's sheep. I thought there was nothing more I could do, but then...

—Then what?

—I saw four or five pigs heading toward the barn where Sizzy nursed her kittens. I ran over, killed two pigs, and scared the others away, but it was too late. They'd injured Sizzy and killed almost all her kittens. All except one—the one I have on my back. His name is Kit-Ten. I don't know if that's really his name, but that's what I call him.

—That's a very sad story, yeah —I admitted—. But believe me, naming things isn't your strong suit.

—Before she died, Sizzy made me promise to take care of him —the dog continued, ignoring me—. So I kept my promise up until now. But I'm telling you, Watson: I don't know how to take care of a kitten. I wasn't born to care for kittens. I was born to herd sheep. Can you understand that?

—Oh, I understand perfectly. But there's something you don't understand either: I'm a male cat. What we male cats do is roam around and sleep, and once in a while, we mate with females. The ones who take care of the kittens and feed them are the females.

—So… you won't be able to help me?

—Mmmm… I'm interested in that human shelter thing. If that's true, maybe I can find a new human to adopt me and feed me.

—Well, I know how to get to that place!

—Really?

—Yeah! It's near a bridge up north. My master and I went there several times. Before the zombie thing, of course.

—Alright, then we'll take care of the kitten together. And in return, you'll show me that shelter with the healthy humans.

—Deal! —the dog said with such enthusiasm that it startled me—. Now, get ready, Watson. We've got a long and tough journey ahead!

And boy, was he right.

CHAPTER 6

FISHING DAY

So, without much fuss (we cats are decisive when we want something), we set off toward the place where the last humans were supposedly taking refuge.

According to Rex, it was far, *very* far, but he couldn't say exactly how far. That was the first red flag. The second was that he talked a lot. In fact, that dog wouldn't stop chattering. And for me, like all cats, constant talking is annoying—we prefer silence and to focus on our own, often unfathomable, thoughts.

In less than an hour, the dog had told me his entire life story: where he was born, who he played with, the names of his sheep, what they did, how they smelled, what time they woke up, what they ate, and a long, tedious etcetera.

After two hours of walking, I was exhausted. And not just from the walk, but mostly from the dog's endless chatter.

We reached a large park and stopped to drink from one of the fountains. The water tasted awful, but it was that or stay thirsty for the rest of the day.

—I think we should rest a bit —I suggested—. Get some food, and...

—Shhh.

I looked at Rex in surprise. He was near the edge of the water, his snout almost touching it. He looked like he was about to dive in.

—What's the...

—*Shut up!* —the dog whispered.

Curious, I obeyed. After a moment, Rex gave a quick thrust, plunged his snout into the water, and pulled out a huge fish, flailing desperately between his teeth.

—*Damn!* —I gasped.

Rex dropped the fish on the grass and looked at me, smiling.

—Now we've got something to eat.

—Where did you learn to fish like that?

—We had a stream on the farm, and every day I'd catch a catfish. My mom taught me how to do it... who learned from my grandpa, and my grandpa from my great-grandpa, and my great-grandpa...

—I get it, I get it... —I looked at him, hesitant, and then asked something I never thought I'd say to a dog— Would you teach me how to do that? I tried hunting pigeons, but they always flew away before I could get close.

—It's easier to catch fish —Rex laughed—. They're dumber than pigeons.

—Will you teach me?

—Of course!

And we spent the next while trying to catch fish. The dog taught me how to stand by the water without making a single move and barely breathing. He showed me how to spot the little ripples and bubbles the fish made as they approached the shore. And then, how to make a sudden snap.

After several tries, I finally managed to catch my first fish. I had to get my whiskers wet, which I hate, but the final result was very satisfying. For the first time since my human died, I had fresh food.

—Well, now I'm really hungry. Let's focus on eating our food.

We lay down on the dry grass and devoured the fish. Rex chewed off a small piece and gave it to Kit-Ten, who ate it with his tiny needle-sized teeth.

—Do you think he misses his mom? —Rex asked, watching him.

—Do you miss yours?

—Of course! I just don't remember what she looked like. But I remember her smell. Like she's right next to me.

We kept eating until we were full. All that was left of the fish were the bones and heads, which Rex buried nearby. I asked him why he did that.

—I don't know, all dogs have the habit of burying leftover food.

—Dogs are so weird.

We set off again after a while. The sun had started to set, and there was a scent of smoke and death in the air.

—Hey, Watson, don't you miss your mom?

—I don't remember her at all.

—And your master?

—You mean my human.

—Yeah, that. Do you miss him or not?

—Well, only because I don't have anyone to feed me.

—Just for that? Don't you miss his smell? His words? His touch?

—No, we cats are cold. We don't have feelings.

—Are you sure?

—Positive.

And I walked ahead so he wouldn't notice my eyes had welled up, remembering my longed-for past life.

CHAPTER 7

THE RED EYED MONSTER

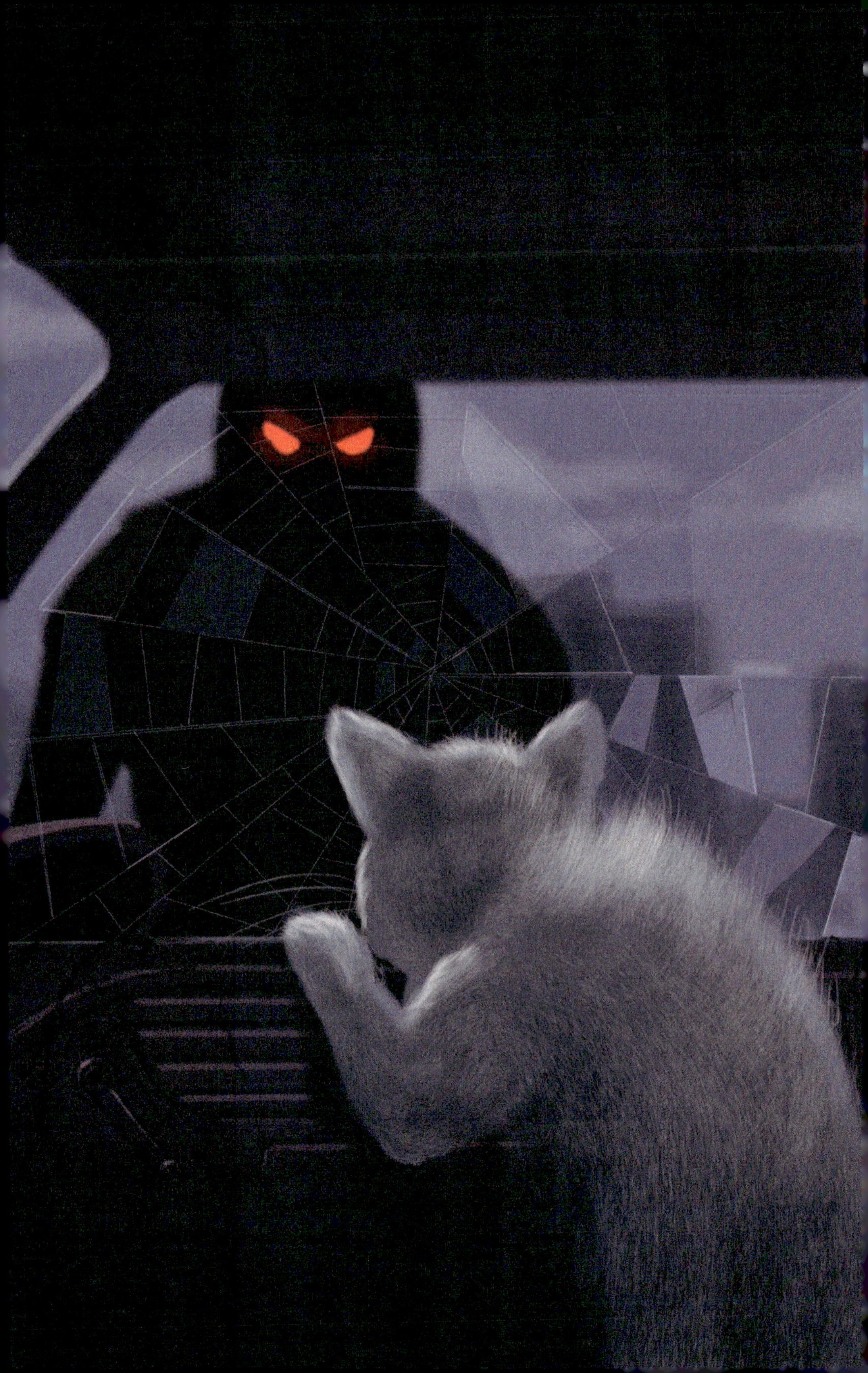

We kept walking until nightfall. Then, Rex said we should stop because it was too cold. I agreed, and we decided to spend the night inside an abandoned car.

It was old and smelled bad, but at least it was warm. The big guy lay down on the back seat, the most spacious spot, and I took the driver's seat. Kit-Ten curled up on Rex's back.

—This kitten sleeps a lot! —the dog marveled—. Ever since he's been with me, all he does is sleep and eat.

—That's just how cats are. You'll have to get used to it.

We fell asleep quickly; the night was cold, and we were exhausted from all the walking.

I thought I'd sleep through the whole night; however, a few hours later, I suddenly woke up. I looked toward the window and saw a horrible face, its red eyes glowing in the dark, staring at us and smiling.

I arched my back and woke Rex with a sharp swipe of my paw.

—What? What? —the dog mumbled, half-asleep.

He saw the figure and began barking wildly. His barks woke Kit-Ten, who, frightened, took shelter under the seat.

—What is that thing? —Rex shouted, terrified—. Why is it looking at us like that?

—I don't know, but it's horrifying!

The red-eyed monster kept smiling at us. It had a vaguely human shape, though its face seemed deformed or something like that. It raised its hand, its long, black nails gliding along the glass. Then, it slipped three fingers through the gap and began rolling down the window.

Rex barked louder and louder. The thing rolled the window down completely and stuck its hand inside; I clawed at it while hissing. Surprisingly, the monster pulled its hand back and moved away until we lost sight of it.

—That was terrifying! It's the most horrifying thing I've ever seen!

—We need to stand guard —I suggested—. Let's rest in shifts, in case that thing comes back.

—Good idea.

So, we took turns for the rest of the night, waiting to see the monster again, but luckily, it didn't come back.

I kept thinking: *What in the world was that?* It seemed like a combination of both a human and a zombie. Or maybe something even worse.

I don't know how, but I eventually managed to fall asleep, and I was plagued by nightmares.

CHAPTER 8

THE KIT-TEEN BATH

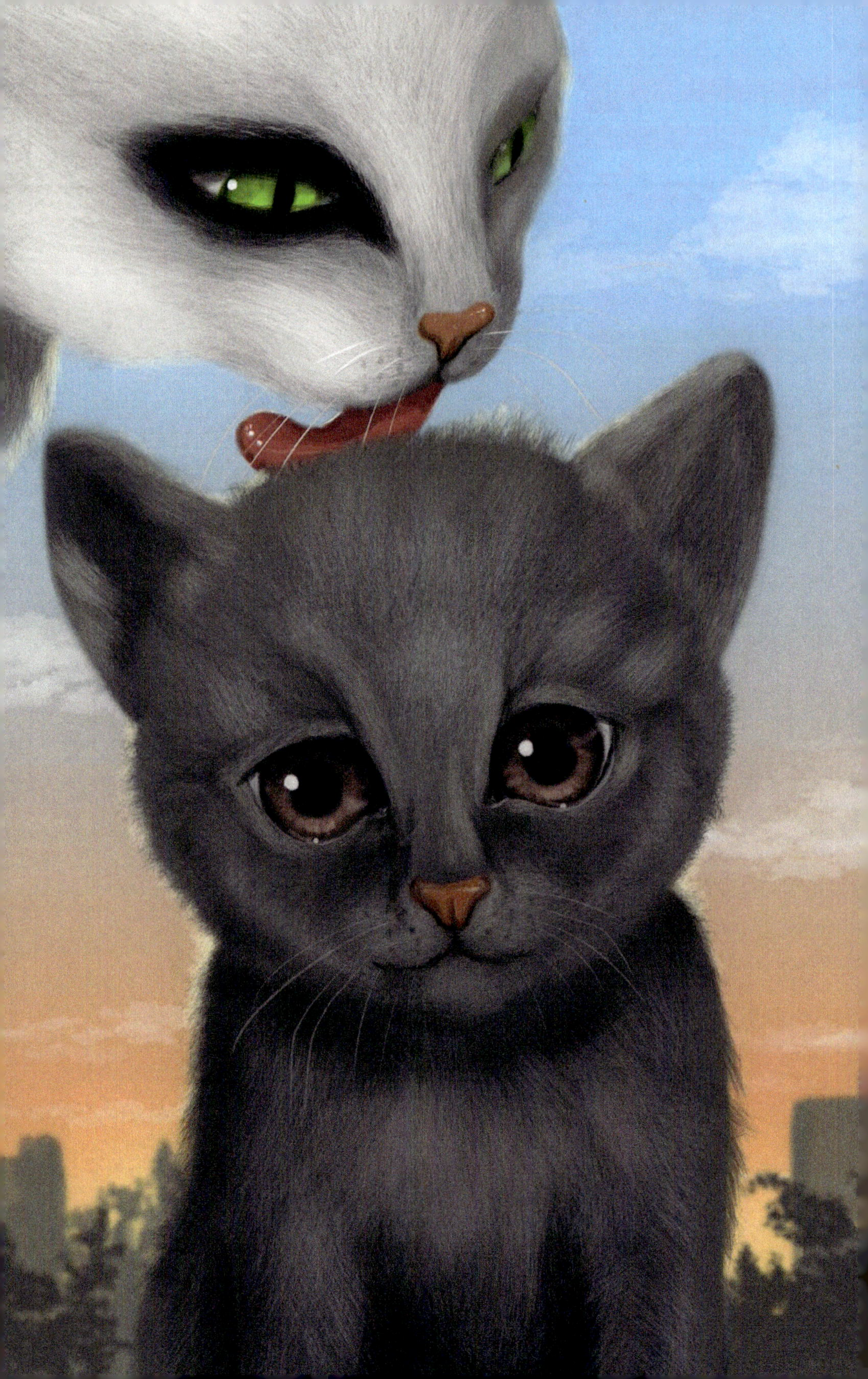

At dawn, I was woken up by something warm and wet on my face.

I opened my eyes and jerked back: it was the damn dog licking me!

—What the hell are you doing!?

—Sorry, it's just... you were sleeping so deeply and not reacting. I thought you were dead, and I got scared.

—I told you, cats sleep a lot. And we hate being licked on the face!

Annoyed and grumpy, I spent a while cleaning the dog's slobber off my face. The kitten, meanwhile, was meowing and circling around the big guy. It was obvious he was hungry.

—I'll go find some food for Kit-Ten —the dog said as he stepped out of the car.

—Wait, what do I do if that thing with the red eyes comes back?

—Just meow. Meow as loud as you can, and I'll come running.

Still unconvinced, I stayed with the kitten.

It was the first time I was alone with him, and I realized he wasn't as annoying as I first thought. His fur was smoky gray, with some darker patches. His big eyes stared at me curiously.

—Just so you know, I'm not your father —I told him, just in case.

I noticed he was dirty. Filthy. Like a dog. I licked him a bit to clean him up. Running my tongue over fur that wasn't mine felt gross, but I kept cleaning him because, honestly, that kitten was disgusting.

When I finished, the kitten gave me a grateful look and rubbed against my head.

—Easy there, Tiger. Don't push it.

However, Kit-Ten didn't seem to hear me and kept rubbing against my body.

—You're happy now that you're clean, huh? Well, of course. It does feel good because you're a cat and you like cleanliness. Not like those dogs that always smell like horse dung —I shot a disdainful glance toward where Rex had wandered off—. But next time, you have to clean yourself. Look, it's easy. Just lick your back, your belly, and your balls. And for the spots you can't reach, wet your paw and that's all—just use it like a sponge...

I spent some time teaching the kitten how to clean himself. And I was so caught up in the task that I didn't notice how long Rex had been gone...

CHAPTER 9

ZOO

ZOOLOGICO

Rex? —I called into the empty street—. Where did you go, you scatterbrained dog?

I didn't say it out loud because I was afraid that monster from the night before would come back. Meanwhile, Kit-Ten looked at me nervously.

—Stay here —I told him—. I'm going to find that dog and see if something happened to him.

The kitten tried to follow me, but I made him stay inside the car. I went out to look for that damn Saint Bernard.

Where could he have gone? If something had happened to him, he would have barked or given that annoying yelp dogs make when they're in pain—the one that sounds like a car slamming on the brakes.

I searched several places: a grocery store, an abandoned building, under a truck.

Nothing.

I was starting to worry. Not so much for Rex but because in his absence, I would have to take care of Kit-Ten. And that idea already drove me crazy.

After wandering around looking for the dog, I arrived at a huge place with a sign that read:

ZOOLOGICAL PARK

At this point in the story, you're probably wondering how a cat knows how to read words. Well, first of all, I'm not just any cat—I'm special. And second, as I've mentioned before, my human read a lot. A lot. Not just Sherlock Holmes books, but also science fiction, fantasy, history, and even natural sciences.

That's how I slowly began to understand some of those strange symbols printed on paper.

I can't read fluently, nor can I read an entire book or even a full page, but I do understand certain words.

Like the one right in front of my eyes:
ZOOLOGICAL PARK

I knew that zoos were places where, in the past, humans kept animals locked up simply to watch them. I could never understand why anyone would pay to see a bored, depressed beast whose only activities were eating and sleeping—or worse, just excreting. But then again, humans had always been strange—almost as strange as dogs. And sometimes, they could also be very cruel.

—Rex? —I murmured, stepping into the place—. Are you here? Still looking for milk for Kit-Ten?

Unless you find a goat and somehow milk it...

I broke off mid-sentence.

The fur on my back stood on end. There was something up ahead—something so terrifying that I instinctively hid beneath some bushes.

It was a gorilla. A massive gorilla, now one of the walking dead. It must have escaped from one of the cages. Its hands, just like its mouth, were covered in blood. Its eyes were crawling with maggots. And yet, it seemed to see through scent, because it lifted its head, sniffing the air repeatedly as if searching for a trace...

And then, with a terrifying roar, it charged straight toward my hiding spot.

CHAPTER 10

ENCOUNTER WITH A GORILLA

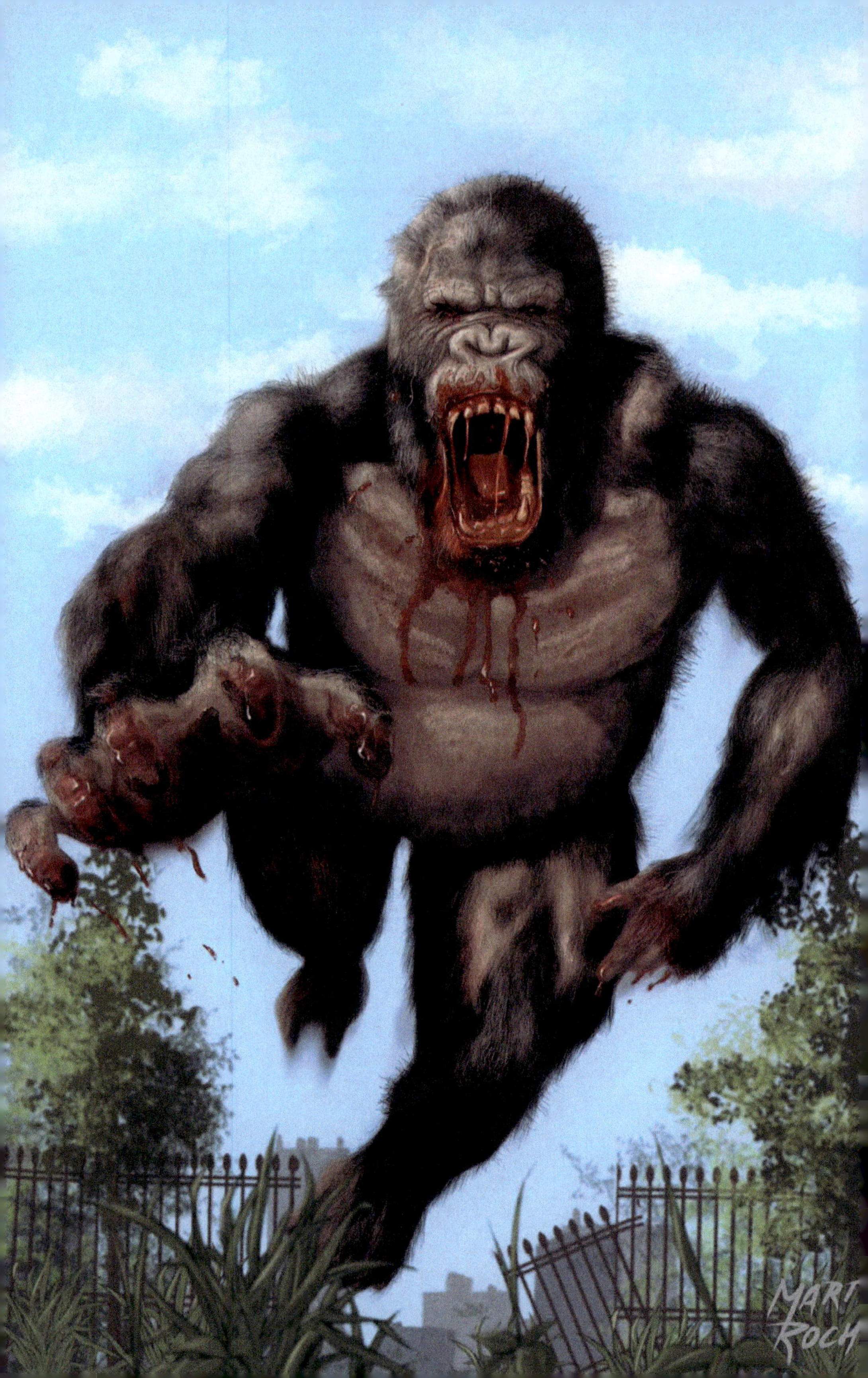
MARI ROCH

I darted out of the bushes and ran. The gorilla was fast and closed the distance quickly. I leapt toward the wall and climbed; my nerves were on edge, and I felt like they were about to snap.

The gorilla jumped as well and managed to brush my tail, almost making me lose my balance.

I ran along the wall. The beast followed from below, stretching its long arms to reach me.

Even in my desperation, I had time to wonder why the gorilla's mouth and hands were covered in blood. Had it had a run-in with Rex? And if so, where was the dog?

I saw the wall interrupted by the branches of a tree; I quickly scrambled onto it. It was an old tree with thick foliage; I felt a bit safer climbing as high as I could through its branches.

A few moments later, I realized my mistake: gorillas could climb too!

My human had read me several books about jungle animals, and I belatedly remembered that monkeys and all their relatives could climb like us cats—or perhaps even better than us.

But it was too late to turn back, so I kept climbing.

The gorilla, down below, jumped and climbed up, swinging from the branches. The animal was huge but agile, its arms were as strong as steel, and its head was the size of a melon. It was truly terrifying; when I saw it, I couldn't help but let out a sharp, terrified meow.

I reached a point where I couldn't climb any higher because the branches were too thin to support my weight. I curled up against the tree trunk, my back arched and my claws unsheathed, ready to fight.

But before the gorilla could reach me, barking echoed from below, catching its attention: it was Rex!

I had never been so happy to see a dog. I might have even let him lick my head a little if he'd asked.

—Come here, big guy! —the dog shouted, bracing both front paws against the trunk—. Pick on someone your own size!

The gorilla let out a deep growl and, fortunately forgetting about me, started to climb down.

—Rex, don't be an idiot, that thing will tear you apart! —I yelled from high up in the tree.

—You think I don't know that? I'm just giving you time to escape, cat. So hurry up!

I didn't wait for him to say it twice: with two jumps, I dropped down to the wall and then to the street.

Had the undead gorilla caught Rex? The dog was too slow to outrun him.

I stopped behind some bushes. My heart was pounding wildly. Time passed, and there was no sound or sign of anything. I began to fear the worst.

Just when I was losing hope, the chubby figure of the dog appeared, running at full speed.

—Run, cat! —Rex barked—. Run for your life!

I turned and we ran. Behind us, the heavy, grotesque figure of the gorilla roared under the bright sun.

Luckily, the beast slowed down after a few blocks, and we managed to get to safety. We stopped behind a building to catch our breath.

—By my masters' mercy! —Rex panted—. That thing was really terrifying—as bad or worse than the red-eyed monster!

—Where were you? —I snapped—. Why did you take so long to return?

—I couldn't find food anywhere. I didn't want to leave Kit-Ten without something to eat… —Suddenly, he stopped and looked at me, scared—. Hey, where's the kitten?

—Don't worry, I left him inside the car.

—You shouldn't have done that! Kit-Ten is very mischievous and never sits still!

Rex bolted toward the car-refuge. I followed reluctantly: that day had been way too hectic, and we cats hate hectic days.

When I caught up to him, I saw the big dog whimpering, his ears drooping.

—By the mercy of the masters, Kit-Ten's gone! —he exclaimed, his eyes brimming with tears—. What have you done, Watson?!

CHAPTER 11

ABOUT CATS' ABILITY TO SEE GHOSTS AND OTHER ABILITIES

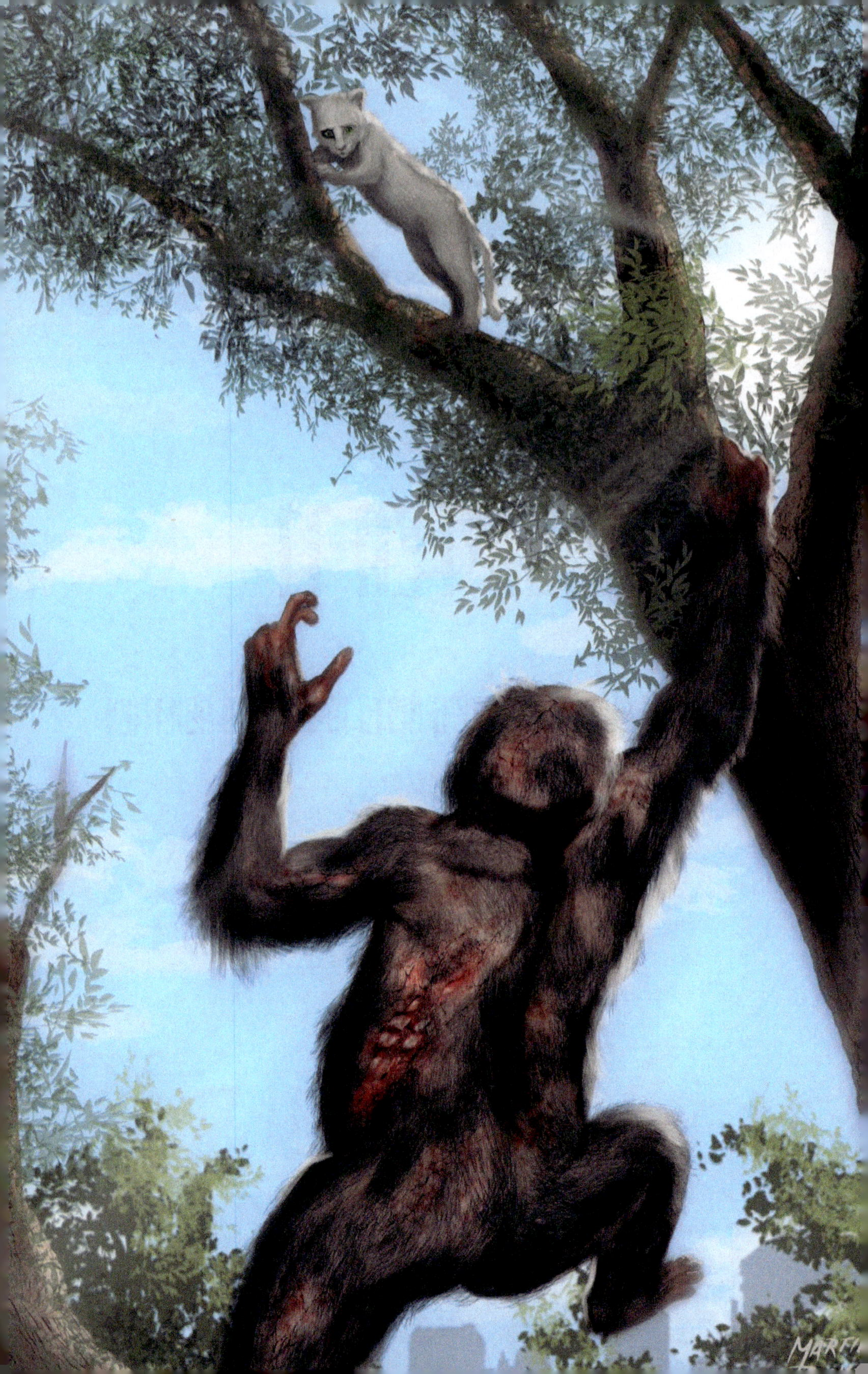

—This is all your fault —I protested—. You took forever to come back!

—It's just... I didn't think that... —Suddenly, the big guy staggered—. I don't feel well. I think I'm going to die!

—What the heck is wrong with you?

—I can't breathe. I can't breathe!

—You're talking nonsense.

But even so, I moved closer to examine him.

Cats have a keen sense for all things related to death, poisoning, illness, bad vibes, and ghosts.

For example, I can tell, just by sniffing someone, whether they're sick or dying.

Once, my human and I visited his sister, and I knew just by her scent that something was eating her from the inside.

Sure enough, the woman died not long after, and my human cried and kept repeating the word cancer.

However, when I sniffed Rex, I couldn't detect any of that. He seemed as strong as me—or like my human before he was attacked by the walking dead. But I did notice his heart was racing.

—You're fine —I told him—. It's just...

—I swear, I'm going to die, cat!

After thinking it over for a few moments, I moved closer to his big head and gave him a hard slap with all my strength.

I barely managed to move his whiskers, but it was enough to Snap the big guy out of his panic.

—What did you do?

—You were hysterical. You were having a panic attack. Simple as that.

—W-what... why... I don't get it!

—My human read a lot of books, even medical ones. And I know what a panic attack is.

—What's a book?

—Oh, for the love of Bast, you're just a clueless farm dog —I rolled my eyes.

Rex kept whining for a bit longer, but eventually, the panic attack passed, and he stared at me, his eyes wide with amazement.

—You cured me! —he said, the big fool—. Your slap cured me!

—No, I only slapped you because...

—Your paws are magic!

—I'm telling you... Okay, fine, you're right, I cured you.

—Thank you! Thank you so much!

He tried to lick me in gratitude, so I pulled away.

—Let's forget about my miraculous paws and focus on finding Kit-Ten, okay?

—Yes, yes, you're right...

—I left him inside this car, but he's not here anymore. Still, he can't be far. Can't you track a scent?

—Me? Sniff him out?

—Aren't you a hunting dog?

—No, no, I'm a herding dog. My specialty is herding and guiding livestock. That's what I did on my farm.

—Oh, I see. But you can track a scent, right?

—Not anymore... I can't.

—Damn it, at least try!

—I don't want to! —Rex whimpered—. The smell of death is everywhere... it scares me!

—Okay, okay, calm down. If you can't use your nose, then we'll have to find Kit-Ten with our eyes...

—Alright, yes —Rex said, perking up a bit.

We searched for the kitten nearby—under other cars, in the drains, under the bushes. We even risked entering abandoned buildings. Nothing.

—Kit-Ten! —Rex howled as loud as he could, startling me— Where are you, little kitty?

—You shouldn't do that —I scolded—. You'll alert every zombie in the area. That horrible gorilla might hear us! Or worse, the red-eyed monster we saw last night...

Fortunately, that shut the dog up.

—Now what do we do? —He said, frustrated.

—We're going back to the car where we last saw him.

—Why? What's the point?

—I think I know how to find him. Follow me!

CHAPTER 12

WATSON INVESTIGATES

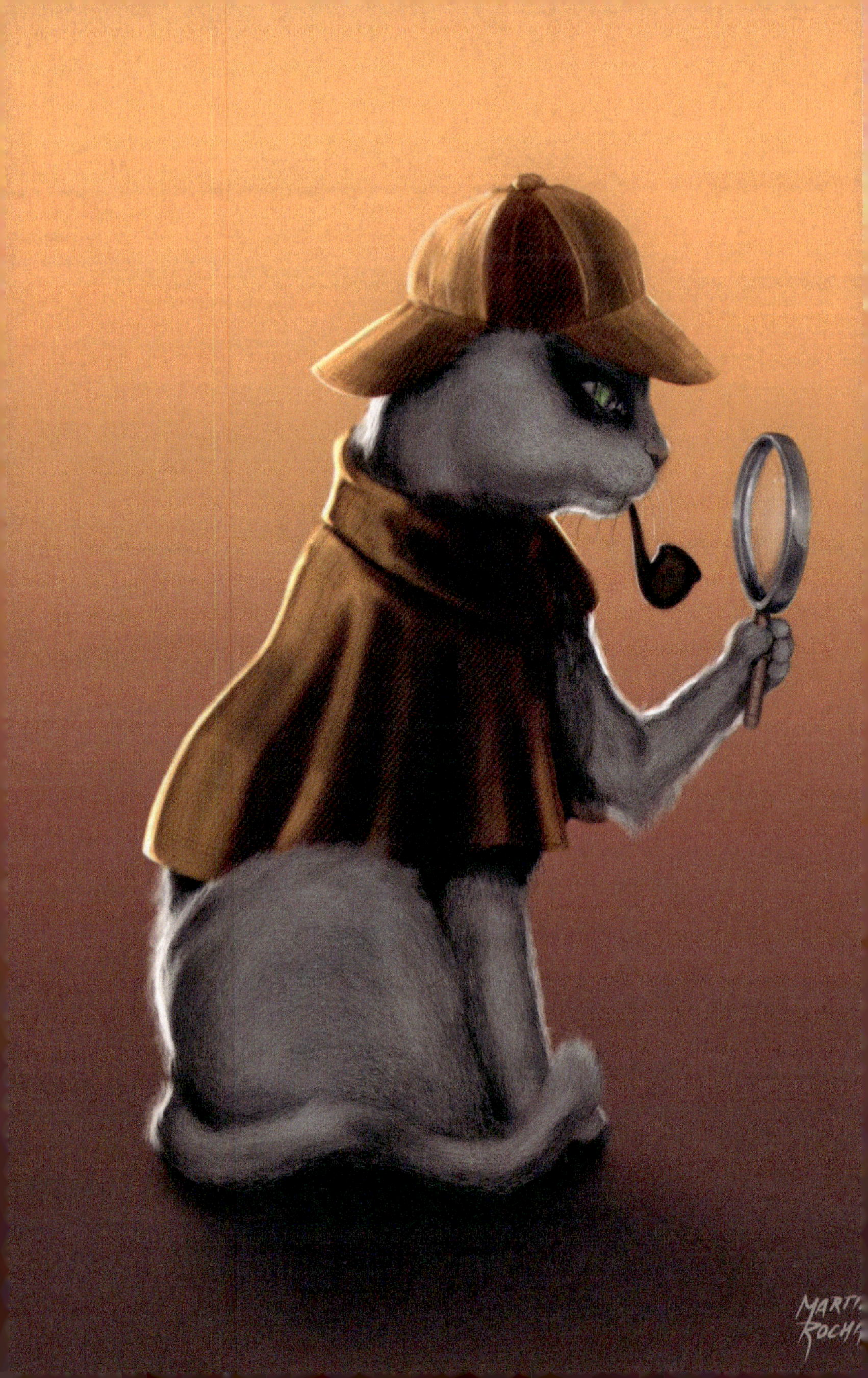

We returned to the abandoned car, which now, under the fading light of dusk, looked gloomy and slightly sinister.

I crawled under the chassis and observed my surroundings. Rex watched me curiously.

—What are you doing?

—I'm investigating.

—Investi-gating?

—Yes, I'm trying to find a clue to locate Kit-Ten.

—And how's that? You know how to do something like that?

I sighed and stopped searching for a moment.

—Ever wondered why my name is Watson?

—Uh… no.

I then explained to him about Sherlock Holmes and his companion Watson, and how, after hearing so many detective stories, I'd come to understand how mysteries were solved.

—The key is observing the scene —I explained—. And a whole lot of thinking.

—Well, I'm looking at everything, but I still can't find Kit-Ten.

—That's because you're missing the other part: deduction. So let me do my job, because I know what I'm doing.

—Alright.

Satisfied with my own explanation, I kept sniffing around under the car.

It turned out to be harder than I thought. I could see and detect many things, but what could they mean?

In the books, Sherlock would spot a man's sleeve stained with soot and deduce he'd traveled on a steam train. But in real life, things weren't so simple!

For example, what could that oil stain under the car mean? It looked fresh, and I was sure I hadn't seen it the night before.

There were also two candy wrappers, one red and one orange. The wind might have carried them there. I also saw an old pen near a wheel, but I had no idea what to make of it.

—Are you done investigating? —Rex asked after a while.

—No —I snapped back.

I didn't want to admit it, but things weren't turning out the way I expected.

I kept looking at the scene, but everything was a dead end, and my head was spinning with a million confused thoughts.

—Are you done? —Rex asked, seeing me restless.

—For now, yes.

—Do you know where Kit-Ten is?

—Not yet, but I've made progress —I lied.

—What did you discover?

—I can't tell you. And stop bothering me, you're distracting me!

Night fell again, and we settled down to sleep in the abandoned car. We were both feeling down.

To make things worse, a cold fog settled in, and the moon was hidden behind clouds, plunging the night into complete darkness.

We didn't want to say it out loud, but we were both afraid for Kit-Ten's life. We didn't know if he'd survive until morning.

—I promised —Rex whimpered—. I promised Sizzy I'd take care of her son. And now he's gone!

—Don't worry, we'll find him tomorrow, I promise.

I felt heavy-hearted and guilty. I could barely sleep.

Near dawn, while Rex was sleeping soundly, an idea hit me like a lightning bolt. It was so sudden and clear that I leapt onto the seat and let out an excited meow.

—What? —Rex said, waking up startled—. What happened? Is the gorilla back? Or the red-eyed monster?

He lunged into the darkness at an imaginary enemy, and I had to stop him.

—No! There's no gorilla, and the red-eyed monster didn't come back. I just thought of something!

—Something about what?

I stepped out of the car and showed him the pen by the wheel.

—Look, this thing still works! It's not oil—it's ink!

—Uh-huh, and? —Rex looked at me, his face still groggy.

—I know what happened to Kit-Ten.

The dog instantly perked up.

—What happened? Tell me!

It was my moment of glory. The moment I had always dreamed of ever since my human read me those fascinating Holmes stories.

But I couldn't announce my discovery in such a plain and simple way.

So I calmly sat back on my haunches, half-closed my eyes, and, puffing on an imaginary pipe, solemnly announced the following:

—Kit-Ten was taken by some humans. But not the dead ones—the ones still alive. There are several, at least two: one is a child, the other is an adult, probably a man, wearing a shirt. They probably passed by here and saw him or heard him meowing. The child might have insisted on taking him, and the adult picked him up. And they went north. So we'll have to travel that way until we catch up with them.

Rex's jaw dropped as if his jaw had lost all strength.
—How… how do you know all that?
—Elementary, my dear Rex —I said, licking my paw.

CHAPTER 13

THE TURTLE

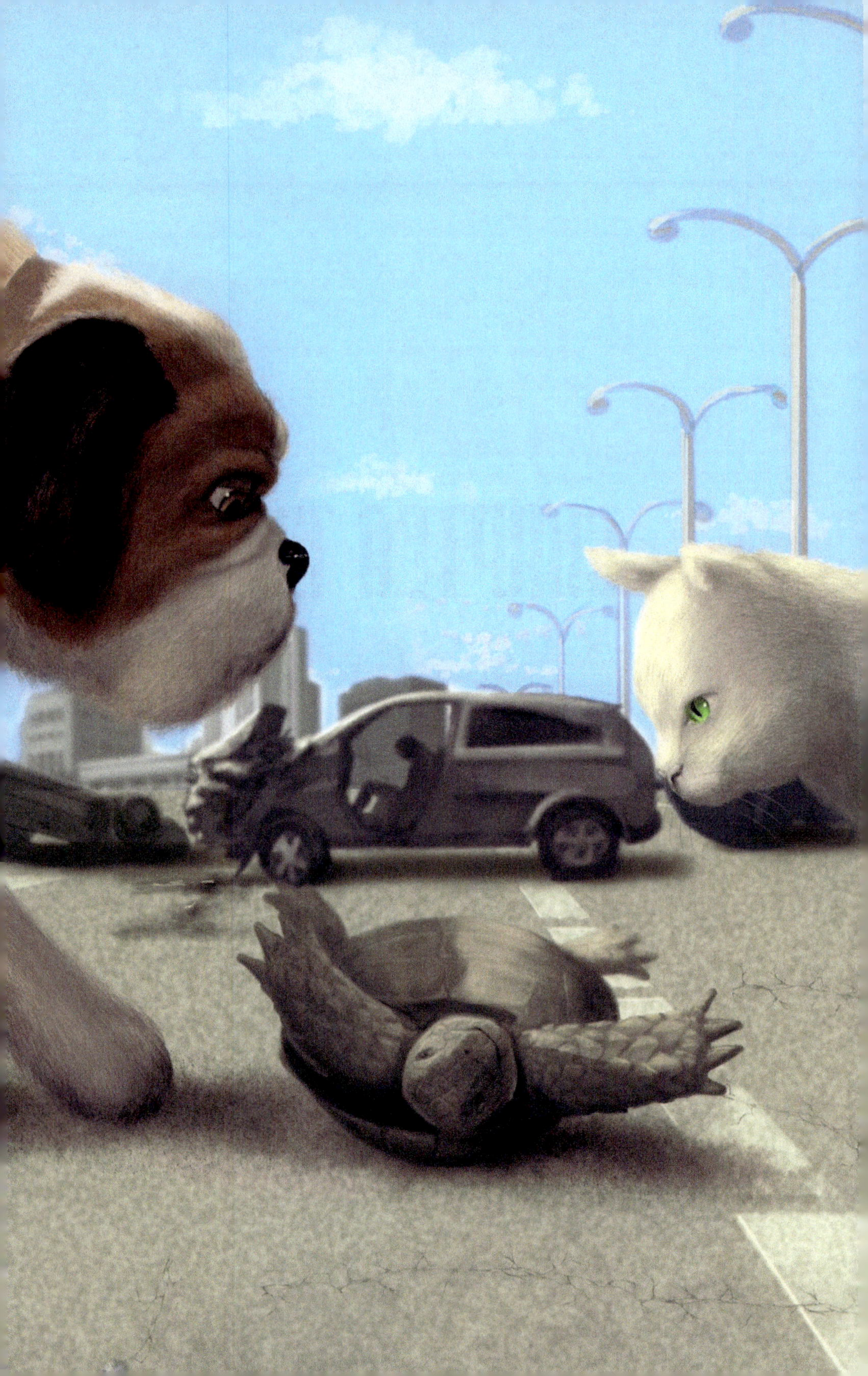

There wasn't much time to lose if we wanted to catch up to Kit-Ten, so we set off immediately.

The early morning was getting colder. Our breaths came out in puffs of vapor.

Rex followed me anxiously:

—How did you figure all that out? —he kept asking—. About the kid, the adult with the shirt, and that they went north?

Wanting to keep him in suspense a little longer, I didn't say anything.

Dawn broke, and we reached a place where the street widened into a long open stretch. There were overturned, crashed, and shattered cars everywhere. And inside each of them, dozens of dead humans.

There were also the other kind—the almost-dead—who stood still, staring at who knows what.

The place reeked of death and destruction. It was like a giant open-air tomb.

—I recognize this place. We passed by here hundreds of times —Rex said, looking at the disaster and whimpering—. My owner used to put me in the back of the truck, and I was so happy.

I pointed with my paw toward one of the road signs:

—This highway goes north. We're on the right track.

—You can read too? —Rex asked, amazed.

—Of course. I can do a lot of things, you'd be surprised.

We kept walking on the asphalt, weaving around the cars and the almost-dead.

After a while, something caught Rex's attention, and he started wagging his tail. I got closer: it was an old turtle, flipped on its back.

—What could have happened to it? —Rex asked.

—Maybe someone kicked it and left it like that.

—Who?

—How should I know?!

—Could you stop talking and help me out here? —the turtle interjected, clearly annoyed.

—Oh, yes, sorry —Rex quickly apologized, always eager to help.

He flipped her over with his snout, and the turtle looked at us while rocking back and forth.

—What happened to you? —I asked.

—One of those damn zombies. It walked past me and kicked me! I thought I was going to die here.

—What's your name? —Rex tried to find out.

—My name is Van Helsing. I'm eighty-four years old, or something like that.

—Have you seen any humans pass by here? With a kitten?

The turtle looked at Rex with tired, somewhat mocking eyes.

—Some humans with a kitten… Yeah, I think so. It was yesterday afternoon. I yelled at them to help me, but those bastards didn't listen.

—Was the adult human wearing a shirt, by any chance? —Rex looked at me, doubtful—. My friend here is sure he was.

—Well, now that you mention it… Yes. He was wearing a shirt the color of blood.

—I told you! —I meowed excitedly—. I told you my deductive method works!

—I'm really impressed —Rex admitted.

—We have to keep going, or we'll never catch up to the humans.

—Yes, you're right —Rex said, and we set off again.

We were walking away when the turtle behind us asked something that made the fur on my tail stand on end:

—Hey, why don't you take me along?

CHAPTER 14

RESCUE PLAN

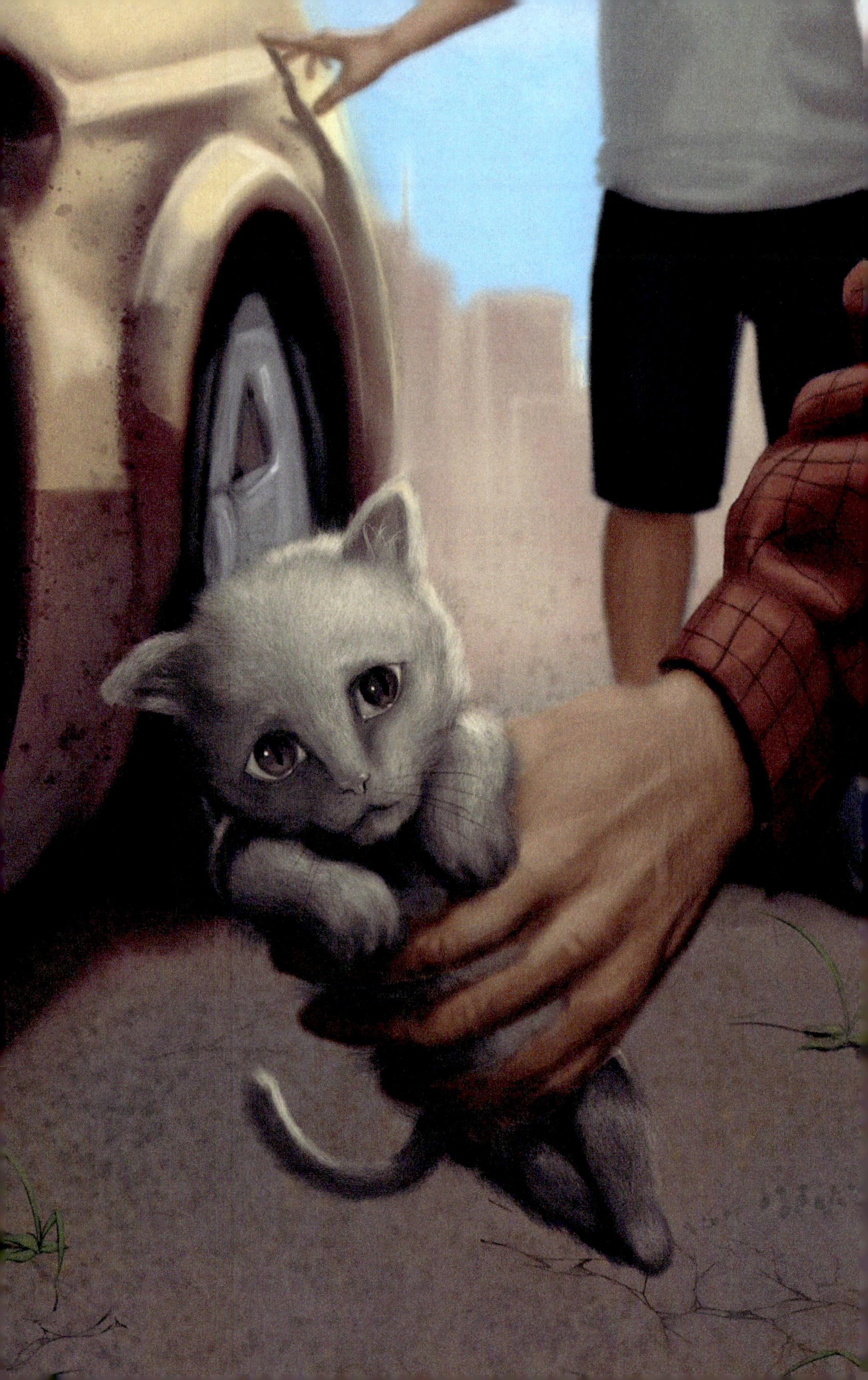

There's no way we're bringing that turtle along. That was the first thing I thought. She'd slow us down and waste our time. Not to mention, she'd be a danger to us, making us slower in case we needed to escape.

However, that big, soft-hearted fool Rex took pity on her. He said she reminded him of a turtle that used to live on his farm. After the zombie attack, he lost track of her, and he'd felt guilty about it ever since.

—For the love of Bast, we can't take every animal we meet along the way!

—Why not? The more of us there are, the stronger we'll be.

—That might be true if we were joined by another big dog like you—or maybe a wolf. But not a slow, old turtle!

—Just so you know, I can hear everything —the turtle interrupted, looking at me with disdain—. Cats think they're better because they're fast and agile. But let me tell you something, Mr. Cat: I've seen many like you—self-assured, thinking they own the world. But then they aged quickly and died. And I'm still here. So you tell me who's the smarter animal.

—For the love of Bast… —I muttered, rolling my eyes in exasperation.

—I hear everything —the turtle repeated—. I'm old, but that doesn't mean I'm deaf or blind. And I notice many things. For example, I know you're after that kitten. And I think I can help you.

—We don't need help from a turtle, or from anyone —I said, licking my paw.

—Oh, no? And how do you plan to rescue the kitten from those men, huh?

—Well... we'll snatch him away.

The turtle pulled back her long, wrinkled neck and seemed to cough. But really, she was laughing. Her laugh sounded like a wheezing seal.

—They won't let you get close. They'll shoot you on sight!

—But... we're friendly! —Rex protested.

—I don't doubt that, Mr. Dog. But humans don't know that. All they know is that there are crazed animals everywhere. The moment they see a dog your size, they'll panic and shoot you right in the head!

I thought that turtle had a point. Still, I didn't want to admit it.

—And what do you propose, if I may ask?

—I have a plan —the turtle let out another one of her strange, dry laughs—. A foolproof plan. You'll be able to rescue the kitten. But for that, you'll need to take me with you.

—And why are you so interested in coming with us?

The turtle's eyes gleamed in a strange way.

—That, Mr. Cat, is something I'll keep to myself. Do you accept the deal or not?

Rex and I looked at each other, and then the dog crouched so the turtle could climb onto him.

—Hop on, turtle. There's always space for one more on my back!

Trust me, it was the worst decision we ever made.

CHAPTER 15

NOSTALGIES

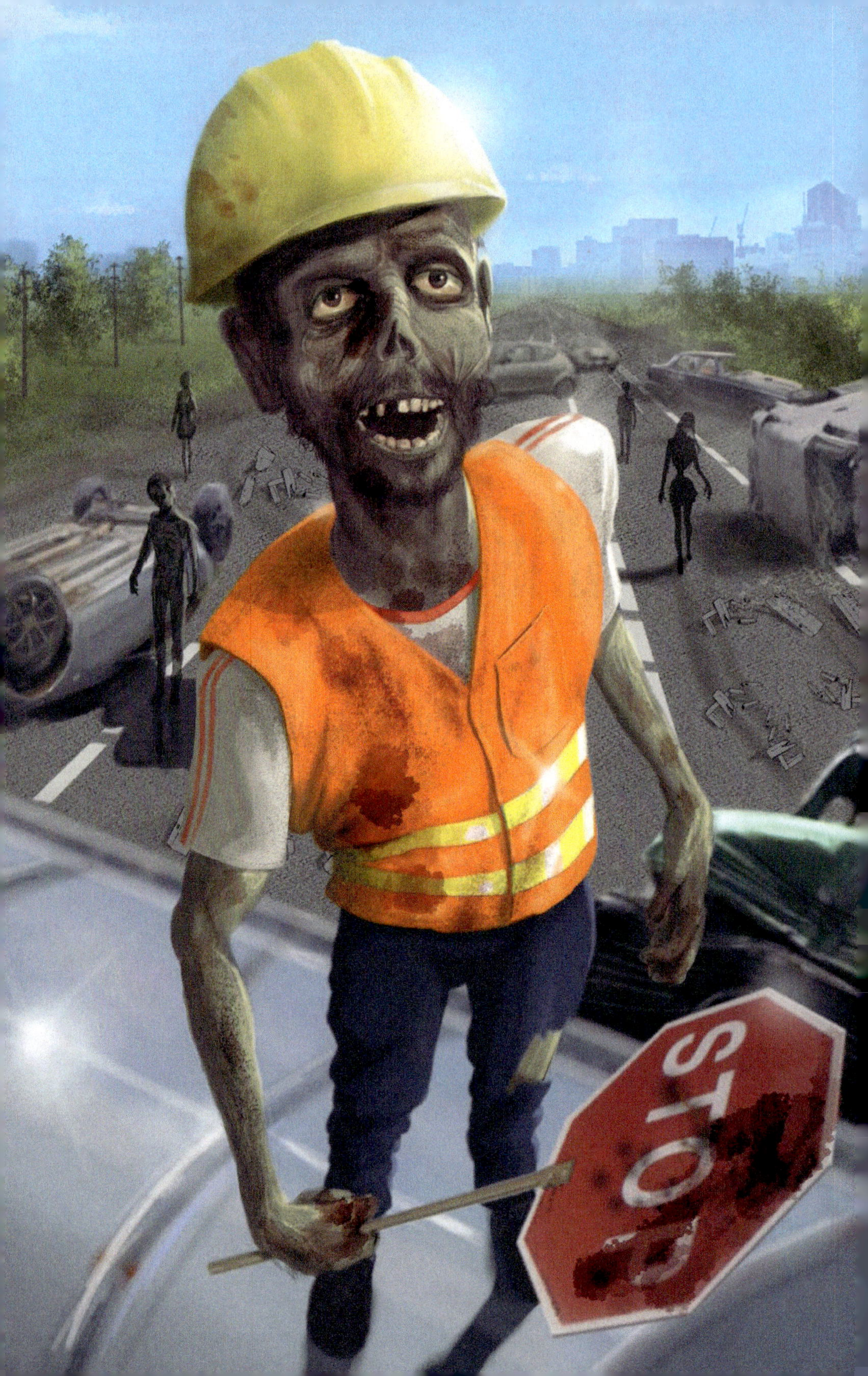
STOP

So, we followed the trail of those humans who had taken Kit-Ten. We walked at a good pace, almost trotting. The sun started to burn, and we stopped to drink from a stream beneath a bridge.

The turtle looked very comfortable on the dog's back. We truly were a picturesque group, bordering on ridiculous: a skinny, wiry cat, a Saint Bernard the size of a bear, and an old turtle clinging stubbornly to his brown leather collar.

We kept moving. Sometimes, the wind shifted, and I could catch Kit-Ten's scent from far away. The dog would get excited and pick up the pace, and I had to slow him down:

—Wait up, Big Guy! Remember, for every step you take, I take seven!

—Uh, yeah, Mr Dog, slow down a bit, or I'll vomit on your head —the turtle agreed, looking pale.

Other times, the wind would change direction, and I'd catch another scent. Several times, I glanced back.

—I think someone's following us.

—Who? —the dog asked, alarmed.

—I don't know. Maybe the gorilla? Its smell is very strange. But it doesn't seem like him.

—Or maybe it's the red-eyed monster we saw that night in the car.

As we moved forward, the congestion of cars, motorcycles, trucks, and even large semis became more noticeable. Most of the vehicles had shattered windows and crushed bodies. Many had crashed into each other, with twisted and even burned metal.

The death toll in that place must've been unspeakable.

—This place makes my paws shake —Rex admitted, sharing my feelings.

After a while, we realized the reason for the traffic jam: two overturned trucks were blocking the road.

There were several zombies wandering around. One of them wore a helmet and a bright orange uniform. For some reason, it was holding an old, blood-stained sign that read:

STOP

—What the hell? —Rex exclaimed.

—I've seen it several times —the turtle chimed in—. Many humans continued their routines after death. I've seen girls with their brains missing sitting behind supermarket counters, pretending to scan groceries. Armless cops whistling at non-existent traffic. Factory workers with dead eyes heading to work with their tattered backpacks. Mangled teachers still giving lessons in empty classrooms. And many more examples.

—But why would they keep doing that?

—I think many still don't know they're dead. And somehow, they try to resume things from their previous lives.

—Wow —Rex said, amazed.

I was impressed too. Not so much by what the turtle said, but by how she said it. Her language was unusually rich and full of peculiar expressions!

—It's because I lived with a writer human for a long time —the turtle explained, hearing my comment—. And writer humans, besides being weird, use very peculiar language that stuck with me.

We left behind the zombie with the yellow helmet. A little further ahead, we saw a dozen or so dead inside a wrecked bus. They were wearing soccer team uniforms and, incredibly, were passing around a rotting ball while shouting garbled nonsense.

—Told you —the turtle nodded—. They try to return to their lives, but I doubt they ever will.

As the afternoon wore on, we kept walking. Rex caught a fish, and we ate it. The turtle, meanwhile, devoured some wildflowers with yellow petals growing in a nearby forest.

As evening approached, we finally spotted the humans in the distance. Eager, Rex ran toward them, but the turtle was surprisingly quick and bit his neck.

—Ow! —Rex yelped, stopping in surprise—. Why are you biting me? Your bite is really strong!

—I told you, Mr Dog, we need to be careful. If the humans see someone your size running at them, they'll get scared and won't hesitate to shoot.

—So what do we do then?

—Wait.

—Wait for what?

—The arrival of the night —the turtle explained—. Humans are practically blind in the dark. That's why they used electric lights. Well, that was before. Now, they use fire.

I was amazed by what the turtle said; I'd never thought of that. Although, of course, I hid my admiration well—I didn't want that creature thinking she was something special.

—And what will we do when night comes? —Rex wanted to know.

—It's simple —the turtle's round, black eyes gleamed again with that strange light—. We sneak in, steal Kit-Ten... and after that... we kill the humans.

CHAPTER 16

ALIENS

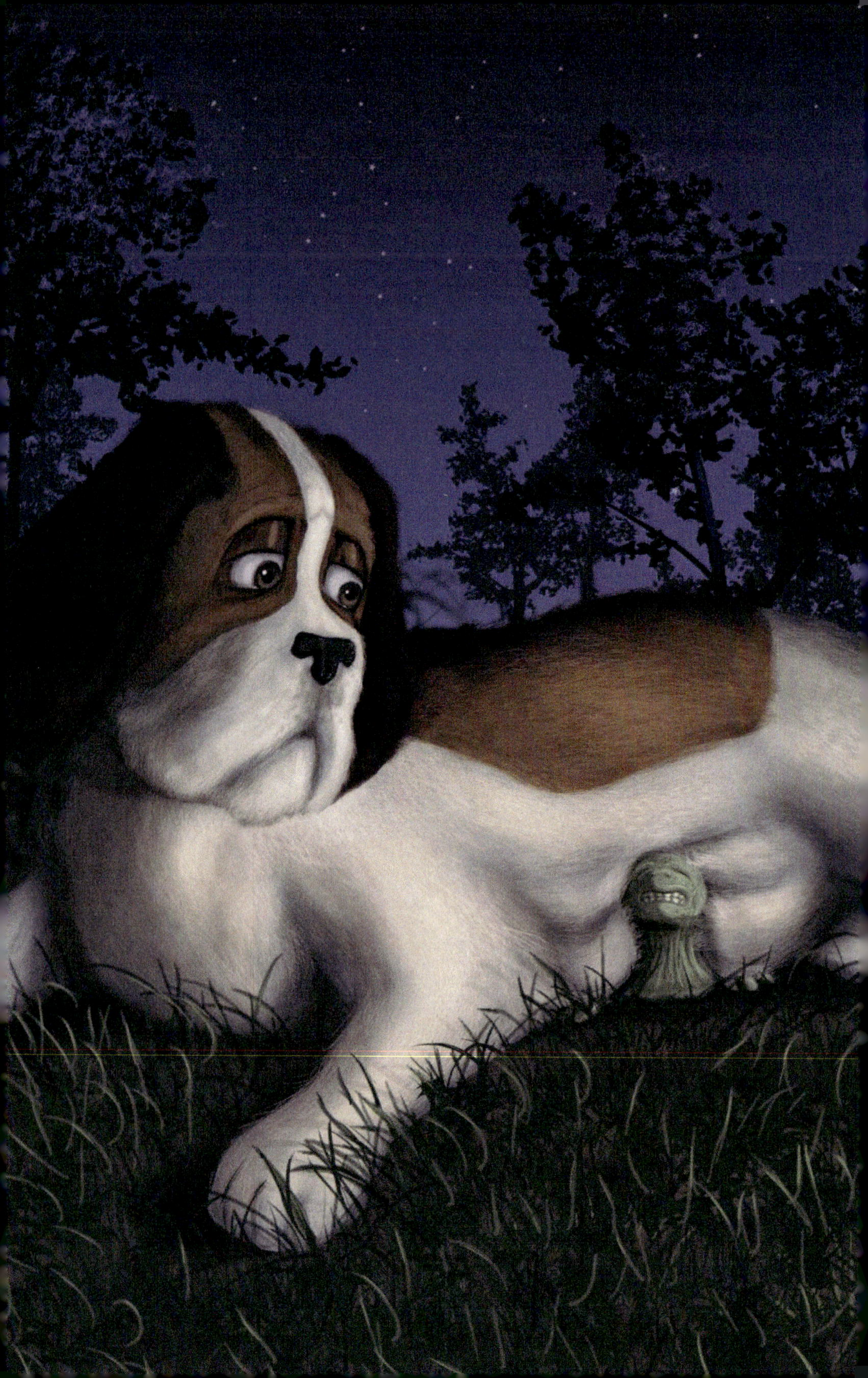

—You're crazy, aren't you? —I snapped, my back arched—. Or are you joking?

—Do you have a better idea, Mr. Cat?

—We're not going to kill any humans!

—Why not? The dog could do it.

—What?! —Rex yelped, scandalized.

—He could sneak up while they're sleeping. Tear their throats out. And then we take the kitten.

I swear, if she had hands, she'd be rubbing them together in excitement.

—That's why you came with us, isn't it? To see a massacre!

—Why do you want to kill the humans?

The turtle's eyes narrowed into thin, dangerous slits.

—Because they're horrible. Evil, wicked beings. I was passed from hand to hand and never happy. First, I was imprisoned by some human pups who always fed me lettuce. Lettuce! When there were so many other things I could've eaten—tomatoes, strawberries, watermelon, and so much more! But no: lettuce every single day. I nearly starved to death with them! Then, that writer kept me captive for thirty years. Thirty damn years! I was sick of seeing him sitting in front of his absurd typewriter, writing God knows what nonsense. And when I finally managed to escape him, this zombie epidemic broke out, and I had a terrible time. I got kicked, mistreated, even nearly run over by a car! —The turtle paused to catch her breath after her heated rant and shook her head—. If I could, I'd kill them all.

—Easy there, Rambo.

—Well, I'm not going to kill any humans —Rex said, crossing his paws—. Especially not ones who haven't done anything bad to me or my friends.

—Fine —the turtle said, clearly disappointed—. Then we'll go with plan B, which is to sneak up while they're asleep and take the kitten. Without killing anyone.

—Well, I like that plan better —Rex nodded.

—Perfect. Now that we've clarified things, I'm going to sleep —the turtle announced.

And she tucked her head inside her shell.

—What?! —Rex and I said in unison.

—You heard me —the turtle's voice echoed from inside her shell—. It's gotten cold, and I need to sleep.

—You're not going to abandon us right now!

The turtle poked her head back out and looked at us, annoyed.

—It's clear you don't understand that I'm cold-blooded. And when the temperature drops, I get sluggish and fall asleep. It's not something I decide—it's in my genes!

—And what happens if we keep you warm? —Rex asked.

The turtle looked at Rex with some skepticism.

—And how would you do that?

—Well… I'll lie on top of your shell. That way, you'll stay warm.

—I'll have to put up with your mammal smell, which isn't exactly pleasant… but fine, I accept.

And so, the turtle was tucked under Rex's sturdy body. Only her head poked out, pointing toward the humans. They had stopped for the night and lit a fire.

—Now we just have to wait for them to fall asleep —she said.

Seeing her neck sticking out of Rex's belly gave me a fit of laughter because it reminded me of a movie about some really bad creatures that burst out of people's stomachs.

—What are you laughing at, Mr. Cat? —the turtle asked.

—Nothing, forget it.

We kept waiting, hidden behind some tall grass by the roadside. The unmistakable smell of roasted meat reached us, making our mouths water.

—What do you think they're eating?

—Rats. And maybe even a dog, or a cat —the turtle said, maliciously.

—Or maybe a turtle —I added.

—Can you see them from here? —Rex asked—. I think you've got better eyes than me, Watson.

I lifted my head above some bushes and spotted, in the distance, seven people: two adult men, three children, and two women. They were sitting around the fire, eating in silence. The guy with the shirt seemed to be the leader. The human pups were fidgeting and playing around. I couldn't see Kit-Ten, though now and then the kids bent down toward a box, and I knew he was inside.

I described the scene to Rex.

—I wish I could bite them all —the turtle said—. I hate human pups. They're especially annoying.

—I agree with that —I admitted.

As the night grew cold, the humans finally went to sleep, and the fire began to die down.

—Now's the time. We have to get closer! —the turtle exclaimed.

We set off. Hidden behind the tall grass, we crept closer until the humans were just a few steps away.

—I'm trembling —Rex whispered.

—Me too —I admitted.
But it was already too late to turn back.

CHAPTER 17

"I WANT TO SEE THE WORLD BURN!"

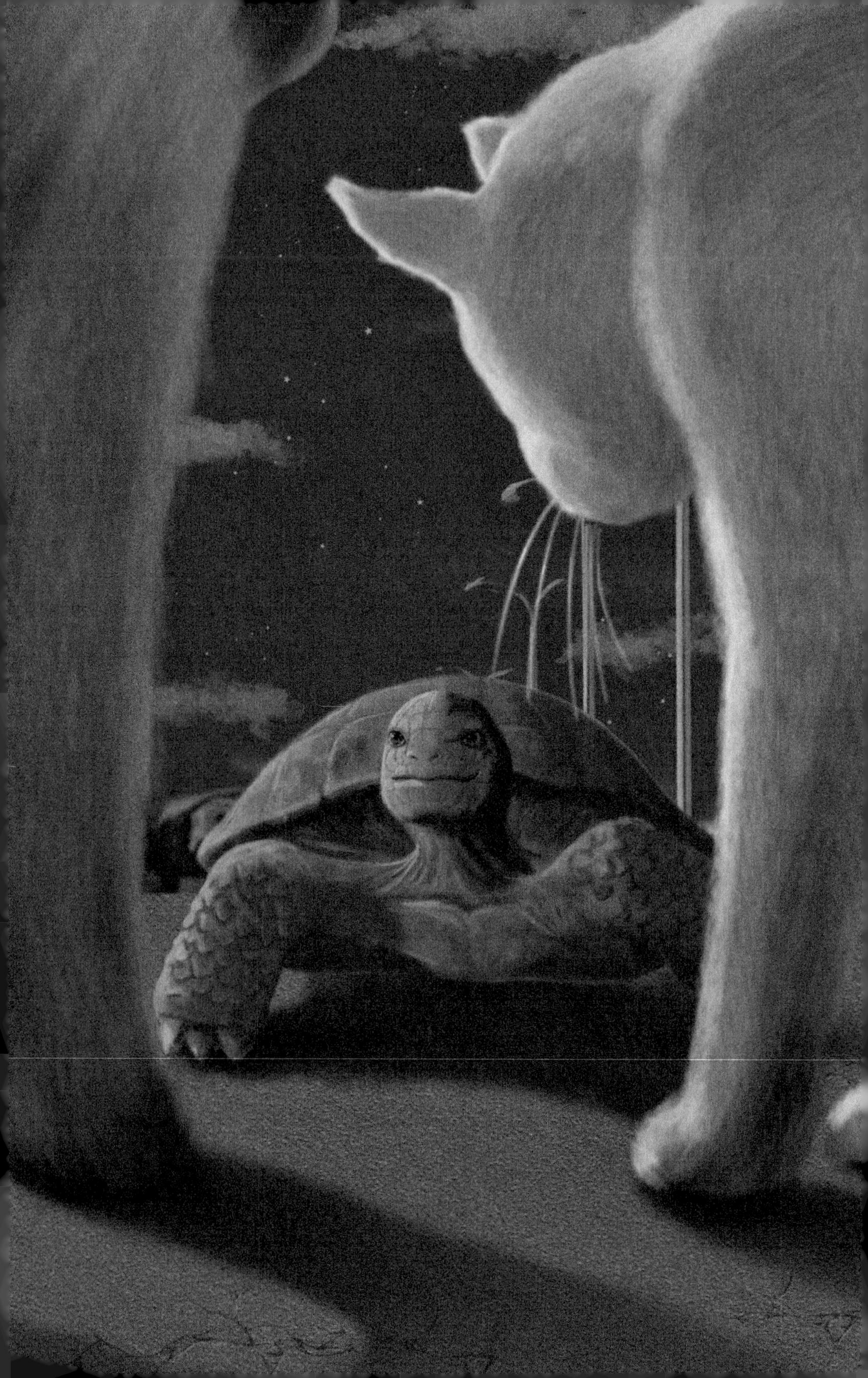

The humans had set up two tents. Bags and backpacks were scattered around. From some of those bags, clothes and cans of food poked out.

We approached the smaller tent: Kit-Ten's scent was coming from there. The zipper was slightly open, and we could see the silhouettes of three human pups—two boys and a girl. Kit-Ten was sleeping, curled up in the girl's arms; he looked content, warm, and safe.

—What do we do now? —Rex whispered.

—Go in and take the kitten —said the turtle, who had settled back on Rex's shoulders.

—Hold on.

Both the turtle and the big dog looked at me.

—What?

—Rex, what did you promise Sizzy?

—Well… that I'd take care of and protect her son.

—And don't you think he's safe enough? —I nodded toward the kitten—. Look at him. He's there, being cared for by a human pup. Kids are annoying, like the turtle said, but Kit-Ten will be better off with the humans than with us. Humans can feed him and give him water. They'll give him shelter. They could even give him medicine if he ever got sick. Can we guarantee food, shelter, and medicine, Rex?

—But your paws…

—What about my paws?

—You cured me! The other day, you cured me. I was dying, you slapped me, and I got better!

—That wasn't because of that, you dumb dog —I said, swishing my tail—. You were just having a panic attack.

—But your paws…

—That's nonsense! What I'm saying is, we're just animals, and humans could take better care of Kit-Ten.

—Are you suggesting we leave him here?

—Exactly —I nodded.

Rex thought about it for a while. Eventually, his eyes welled up, and he came to the same conclusion.

—I think you're right. It's better if we…

—Forget it! —the turtle cut in, furious—. I didn't stay up all night just for you to change the plan now. I want to see the world burn!

With that, she opened her mouth and bit down hard on one of Rex's ears.

The big guy howled in pain. The human pups woke up. From the neighboring tent, there were noises, and someone shouted:

—Damn it, who's out there?! Show yourself, or I'll kill you!

—What did you do, turtle?! —I hissed in rage.

—Just added a little spice to the situation. Now, grab the kitten and let's get out of here!

But we didn't have time to do anything: within seconds, the adult humans from the other tent charged out, shouting and firing wildly.

CHAPTER 18

ESCAPE INTO THE DARKNESS

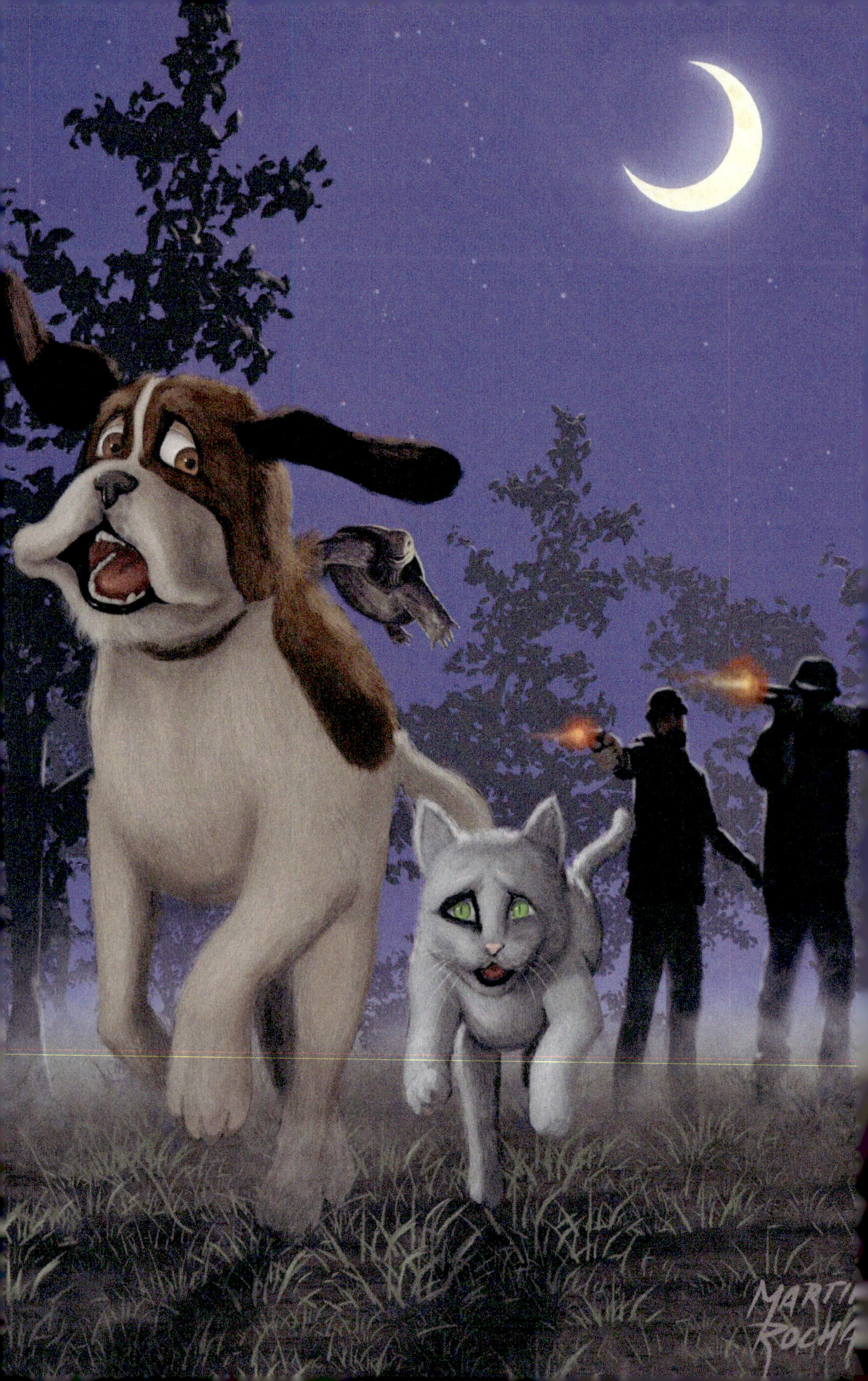

The place very quickly turned into hell. Bullets whizzed by and ricocheted off the asphalt. I leapt toward the tall grass and took cover; however, I was more worried about Rex, since he was much slower and an easier target than me.

The terrified dog froze in place. The men were getting closer, firing relentlessly. I peeked through the grass and shouted:

—Rex, you idiot dog! Move or they'll kill you!

But it wasn't my warning that made him react—it was the shout of one of the women:

—Stop shooting! YOU'RE GOING TO KILL THE KIDS!

The gunfire ceased. Taking advantage of the ceasefire, Rex spun around and bolted. The men threw something at him (I think it was a piece of wood), and it hit him square on the haunches, making the dog yelp.

—Watch out, Rex! —I warned, though it was useless.

The dog caught up to me, and together we bolted into the fields. The gunfire resumed shortly after. A bullet grazed my ear, and warm blood trickled down. Rex stumbled, and moments later, a shot shattered a lamppost just a whisker above his head.

—Kill them! Kill those infected things! —the women screamed.

—But we're not infected! —Rex shouted, though of course, none of the humans could understand him.

They chased us for what felt like forever until they tired out and returned to the camp. We stayed hidden behind some trees, panting and shaking with adrenaline. Rex saw the blood on my ear and cleaned it with a lick.

—It's just a scratch, but thanks anyway —I looked over the dog's back—: Hey, where's the turtle?

Alarmed, Rex twisted his neck only to see that there was nothing riding on him.

—Oh, damn it, she must've fallen off while we were escaping. We have to go back for her!

—We're not going anywhere —I stopped him—. The humans must be on high alert. The moment they hear any noise in the grass, they'll shoot.

—But...

—The turtle can take care of herself. If she's lived eighty-four or eighty-five years without help, she can survive a few more minutes without us.

—I guess you're right.

We stayed put, listening. The humans at the camp were clearly terrified, shouting orders at each other and pacing around. I climbed a tree to get a better view. The human pups were crying, and the women tried to calm them while the men argued among themselves. What a mess we caused!

—All because of the turtle —I reminded the dog—. That damn animal is completely insane!

—Why would she bite me? Why would she want us to fight the humans?

—Because she's nuts. There's no other explanation.

After a while, things quieted down. The humans decided to rest again. But now there was a difference: one of the adults was standing guard. He had a rifle nearly as long as he was tall and patrolled, scanning the grass.

—What do we do now?

—I think it's best if we leave —I suggested—. Trust me, Kit-Ten will be better off with them.

—Yeah, I know —Rex admitted, and tears rolled down his fur—. Still, I'm going to miss him a lot.

We turned around and started walking away. We were just getting further when we heard a gunshot—and then another. And screams. They were coming from the humans' camp; something terrible was happening there.

CHAPTER 19

SURVIVOR

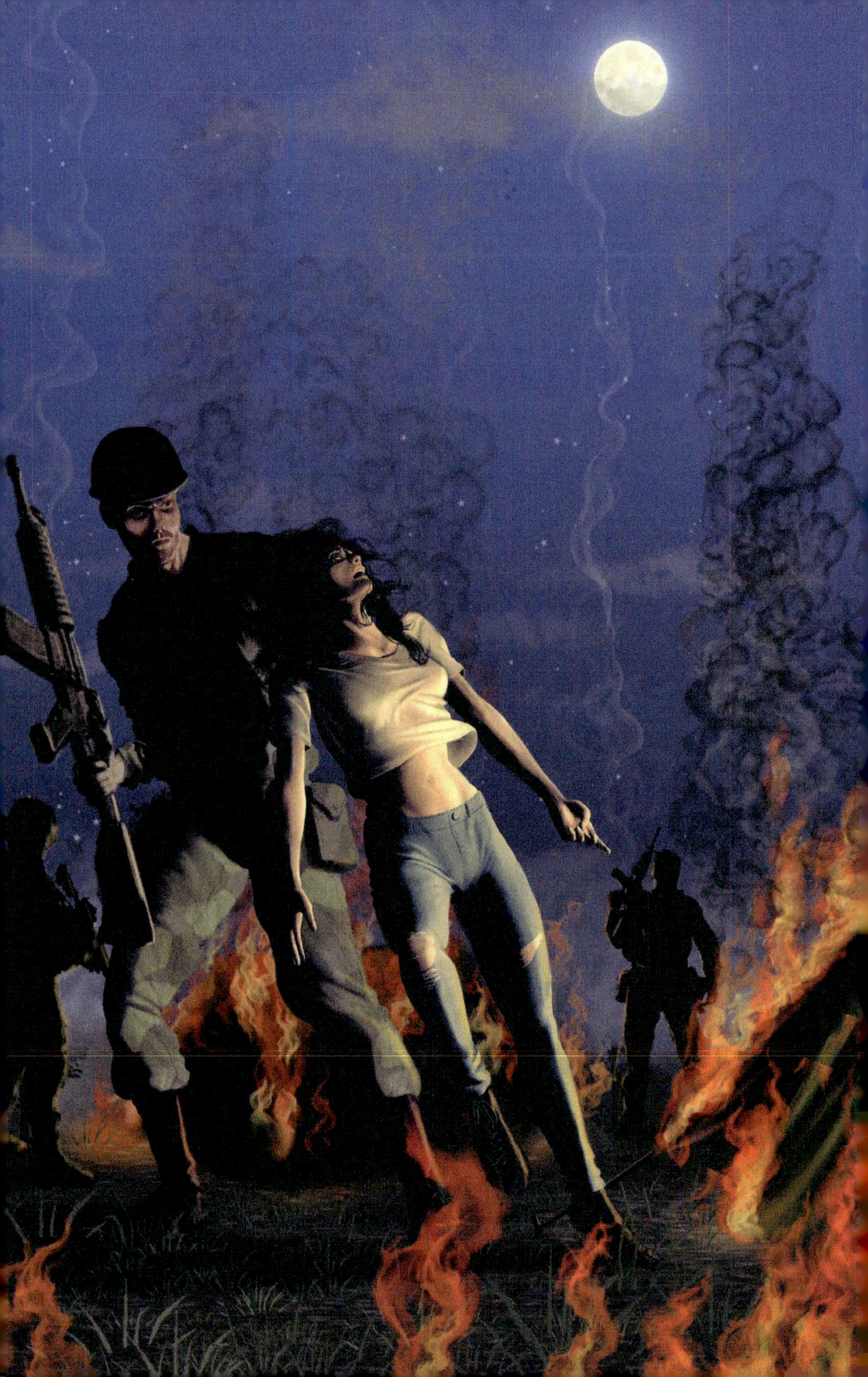

We rushed toward the camp, stopping just a few steps away, hidden behind the tall grass. What we saw horrified us: the camp was under attack. But not by zombies—by living humans who seemed just as violent as the walking dead.

The attackers had killed the two men and captured the women and children. There were about ten of them, all armed with torches and long-range weapons, the kind you'd see in war movies. Their faces were painted red, like ancient warriors.

They ransacked the camp, looted the food, and set the tents on fire. They moved in an old green truck splattered with mud. The prisoners were thrown into the back, and the truck sped off, blaring a horn that left my head spinning.

—By the love of the masters, what's going on? —the dog whimpered.

—Damn them! —I couldn't hold back my anger—. They're killing each other like animals!

—It's in their nature —came a voice behind us, making us jump. We turned around and saw the turtle peeking out from the bushes—. That's why I hate humans. They're savage and aggressive.

—That's not true! —Rex protested, distressed—. The masters aren't like that! They're good and they take care of us!

—You, Mr. Dog, have only seen the good side of them. But believe me, they're worse—especially when their hides are at risk.

—And what will they do with the women and children? Why are they taking them?

The turtle pointed with her head toward the direction the truck had gone.

—Look, they're all men. In times of war, men behave the worst. They'll force the women to breed, and the children... they'll make them work as slaves.

—Look, there's Kit-Ten! —I pointed.

Sure enough, the kitten was meowing desperately inside a box, perilously close to the flames. The fire was closing in fast. Without hesitation, Rex leapt into the fire to save him.

He returned moments later, Kit-Ten between his teeth, his fur singed but relief shining in his eyes.

—Oh, Kit-Ten, I'm so happy to see you again! —he said, placing him on the ground and covering him with sloppy licks—. I swear from now on, I'll take better care of you...

—Listen —the turtle interrupted, her voice tense—. Do you hear that?

We paused our celebration to listen. Over the crackling of the flames, we could hear a long, broken sobbing. It was coming from the tall grass nearby. Cautiously, we approached and found the source: the human pup—the girl—who had apparently managed to escape the attack. She was sitting on the ground, crying inconsolably.

CHAPTER 20

PUPPY

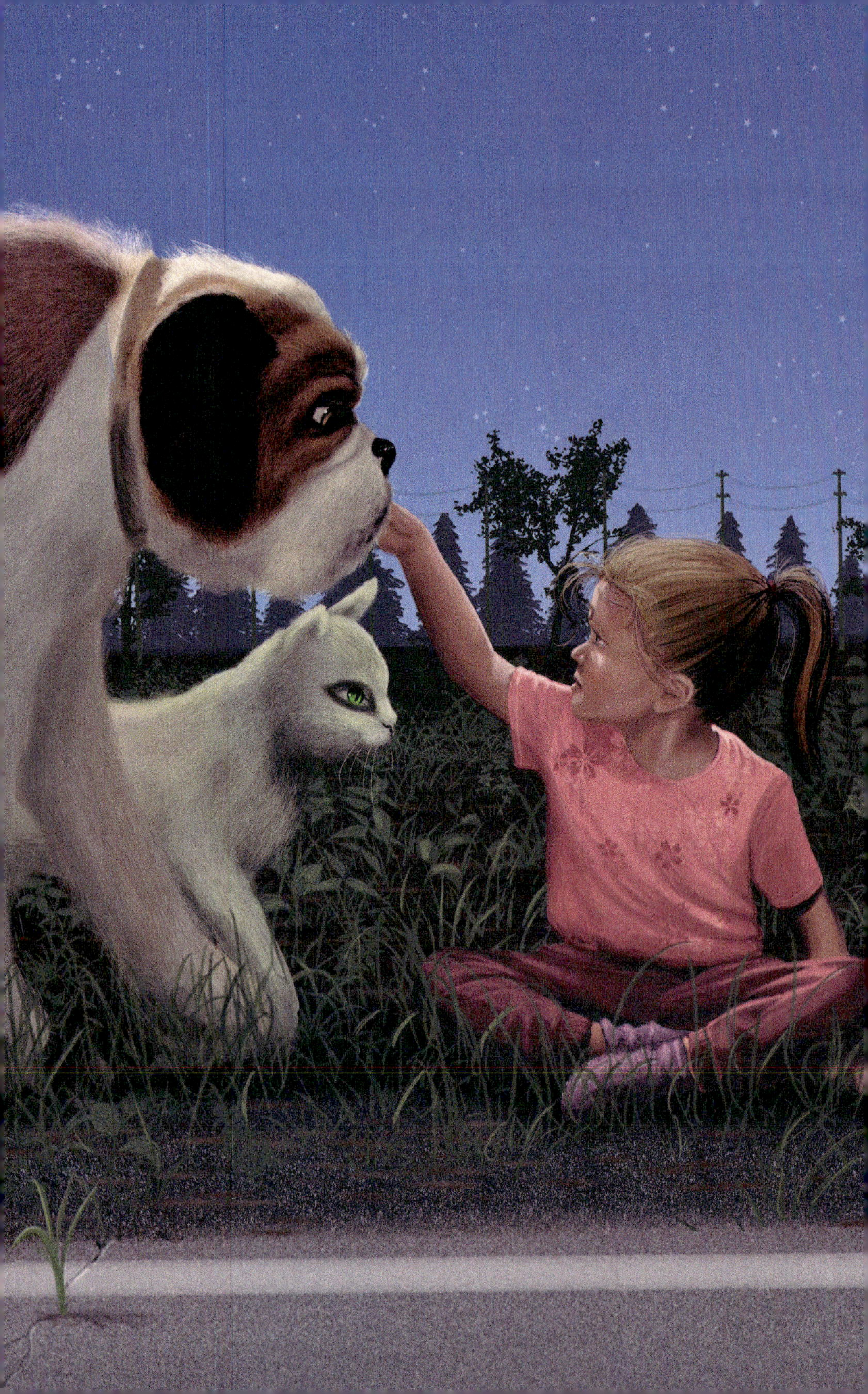

She was a little girl, about three or four years old. She wore a pair of pink pajamas, dirty and torn. When she noticed our presence, she stopped crying and looked at us with wide, astonished eyes.

—Hello, little girl —Rex stepped closer.

The human pup started crying again.

—You total idiot! —I hissed—. Humans can't understand you. You'll only scare her!

After a while, the girl managed to calm down and stroked Rex's snout. Then, she tried to touch the turtle, who immediately retreated into her shell.

—If she touches me, I'll bite her finger off! —the turtle grumbled from inside her shell.

—We have to help her —Rex said—. She's alone and will die if we leave her here.

—WHAT?! —the turtle and I exclaimed in unison.

The dog nodded.

—We have to take her with us.

—But... she must be four years old! —I argued—. She's big enough to take care of herself!

—Humans aren't like cats, Watson. We grow up fast; they take years to mature. Maybe you were a father at 4 years old, but a human at that age is barely more than a baby.

—Oh, come on, this must be a joke! —the turtle and I protested again, in unison.

—And how are we supposed to help a human? —the turtle asked—. We can hardly keep ourselves alive!

—I don't know —Rex said firmly—. But we have to.

It was the first time since I'd known him that he seemed so serious. I realized his instinct to help made him strong, even fearless. I also concluded it would be useless to argue with him.

—Assuming you're right and we somehow can help this human pup, where will we take her? —I asked.

—Well, that's clear: to the humans' refuge. Which is, coincidentally, where we were headed.

—Hold on a minute —the turtle interrupted—. You two want to go to that human refuge? Where supposedly there are healthy people forming some kind of new society?

—Yes.

—That place, further north?

—YES! —Rex said, wagging his tail—. Have you heard about it?

—Of course, I've heard of it. And I'm telling you, it's the worst idea you could have.

—Why?

—Because… they eat dogs. And cats. And any animal that crosses their path.

—No —Rex said—. That's not possible.

—I'm telling you, Mr. Dog, it's true. Look around you! People are killing each other over food. Do you really think they wouldn't kill a dog or a cat? Or even a turtle...

—I refuse to believe that —Rex said, lowering his ears—. My master is there, waiting for me. What you're saying isn't true, turtle!

The dog lifted his face toward the cloud-covered moon and let out a long, mournful howl that gave me goosebumps and made me pity him.

—Well, I'll just say this: you can go wherever you like —the turtle said—. But I won't go there. And even less with this… —She glanced at the girl, who was still silently watching us— … daughter of the devil.

With that, she turned around and headed into the forest.

—Good, better for us! —I meowed furiously—. Go! Leave, and never come back! You've done nothing but cause trouble!

—I just did what I had to do —the turtle said without turning around—. Sooner or later, you'll remember my words. And you'll regret not listening to me.

She passed under some branches and disappeared from our sight.

I placed a paw on Rex's back.

—Relax, that turtle doesn't know what she's talking about.

—Of course, she doesn't! She's never been there, she's just an evil, lying turtle!

—Of course, Rex, of course.

—My master is waiting for me there. I'm sure of it!

—Sure, just calm down. Remember, we need to help the human pup.

That helped Rex regain his composure.

—You're right. We have to take her with us!

—I think that's the best thing to do —I assured him.

But I couldn't stop thinking about the turtle's ominous words: *"They eat dogs. And cats. And any kind of critters wandering around..."*

CHAPTER 27

REX TALKS ON THE PHONE

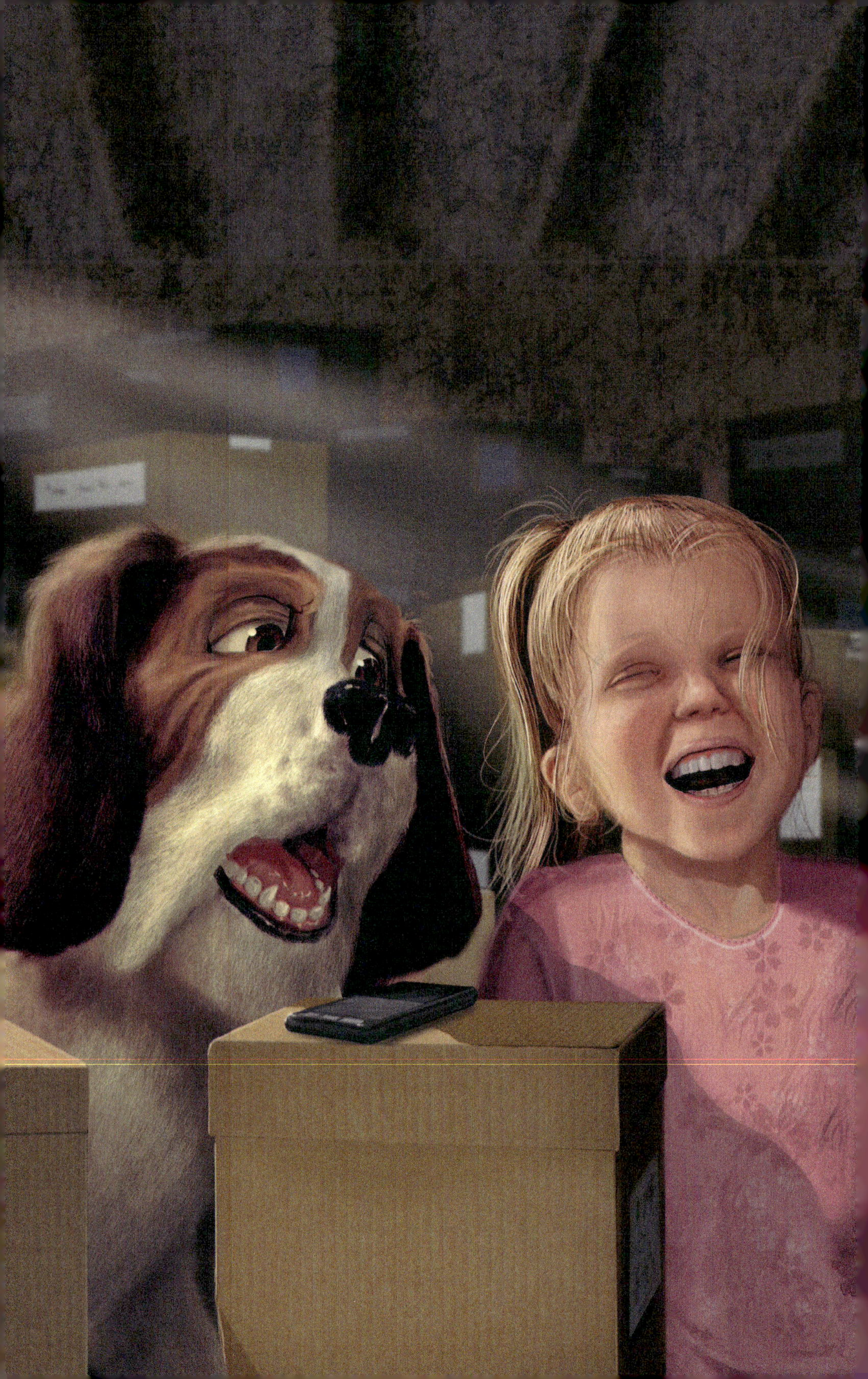

I thought it would be difficult (if not impossible) to explain to the girl that she should follow us. However, all it took was Rex gently tugging on her sleeve for her to stand up, brush the dust off her pink nightgown, and start walking.

—You really have a knack for communicating with humans! —I said in amazement.

—Sometimes, I think that's the only thing I'm good at —Rex confessed, wagging his tail—. But it's enough for me.

The girl was completely fascinated by Rex. She held onto his collar and let herself be guided by him. Me, on the other hand, she barely glanced at, which gave me a profound sense of relief.

We left the burning camp behind and crossed a toll booth that had been turned into a barricade of cars and motorcycles.

—A lot of people must have died here —I observed.

—Don't say that in front of her; you'll scare her.

—And you think she's going to understand me? Humans can't understand animals —I glanced at the girl to confirm my point. She, in turn, looked at me but said nothing—. It's weird she hasn't said a word. Human pups usually talk to dogs and cats.

—That's true —Rex acknowledged—. What could be wrong with her?

—Maybe… she's in shock —I guessed, recalling the old medical books my human used to read.

—In shock?

—It's when someone experiences a very strong emotion. They just killed her parents; imagine how she must feel.

—That could be, yeah. But she doesn't look very nervous.

We kept walking. We passed the toll station and then ventured onto a narrower road. Dawn was approaching, and the girl started to look tired.

—We should stop —Rex suggested.

—Yeah, it's been a long night; some rest wouldn't hurt.

We chose an abandoned truck to rest in. The trailer was packed with cardboard boxes, which fascinated me because, like any cat, I love cardboard boxes.

Rex tore open a few boxes with his teeth, revealing hundreds of mobile phones. He pressed his nose against one of the devices and said:

—Hello, yes? Is this the restaurant? Please send me three thick hams.

—Oh, Rex, you're such a clown —I scolded him.

Then something unexpected happened—the girl burst out laughing. She probably didn't understand a word of what Rex was saying, but seeing a dog bark at a phone must have seemed very funny to her.

—Hello, is Armando there? —Rex got bolder—. No? I'm still with the instructions.

—Oh, by the love of Bast, enough already, dog.

—"Hello, is this the butcher shop?" —Rex continued, ignoring me and watching out of the corner of his eye as the girl laughed uncontrollably—. "No, this is the shoe store." "Oh, sorry, wrong number." "No problem, bring it over, and we'll exchange it."

—I didn't know you were Mr. Comedy... —I tried to protest, but I couldn't hold back a laugh. It had been a while since I'd laughed, and I had to admit—it felt good.

Moments later, the girl surprised us by picking up one of the phones, bringing it to her mouth, and pretending to talk.

We fell silent. Because, instead of words, strange, broken sounds came from her throat, as if they were being pulled from deep in her chest.

—What's wrong with her? —Rex suddenly looked worried—. Why is she doing that?

—I think she's mute. My human had a sister like that. She couldn't talk; she communicated with signs.

We kept watching the girl as she pretended to talk on the phone, mixing guttural sounds with giggles and little breaths. Finally, she seemed to get tired. She looked at us for a moment, then petted Rex's snout. Her small hand touched my tail, and a mysterious smile crossed her lips before she drifted off to sleep.

—She's really beautiful —the dog said, tenderly.

—Don't get too attached —I warned him—. Come on, let's sleep. We've got a long day ahead.

CHAPTER 22

THE LAST CAN

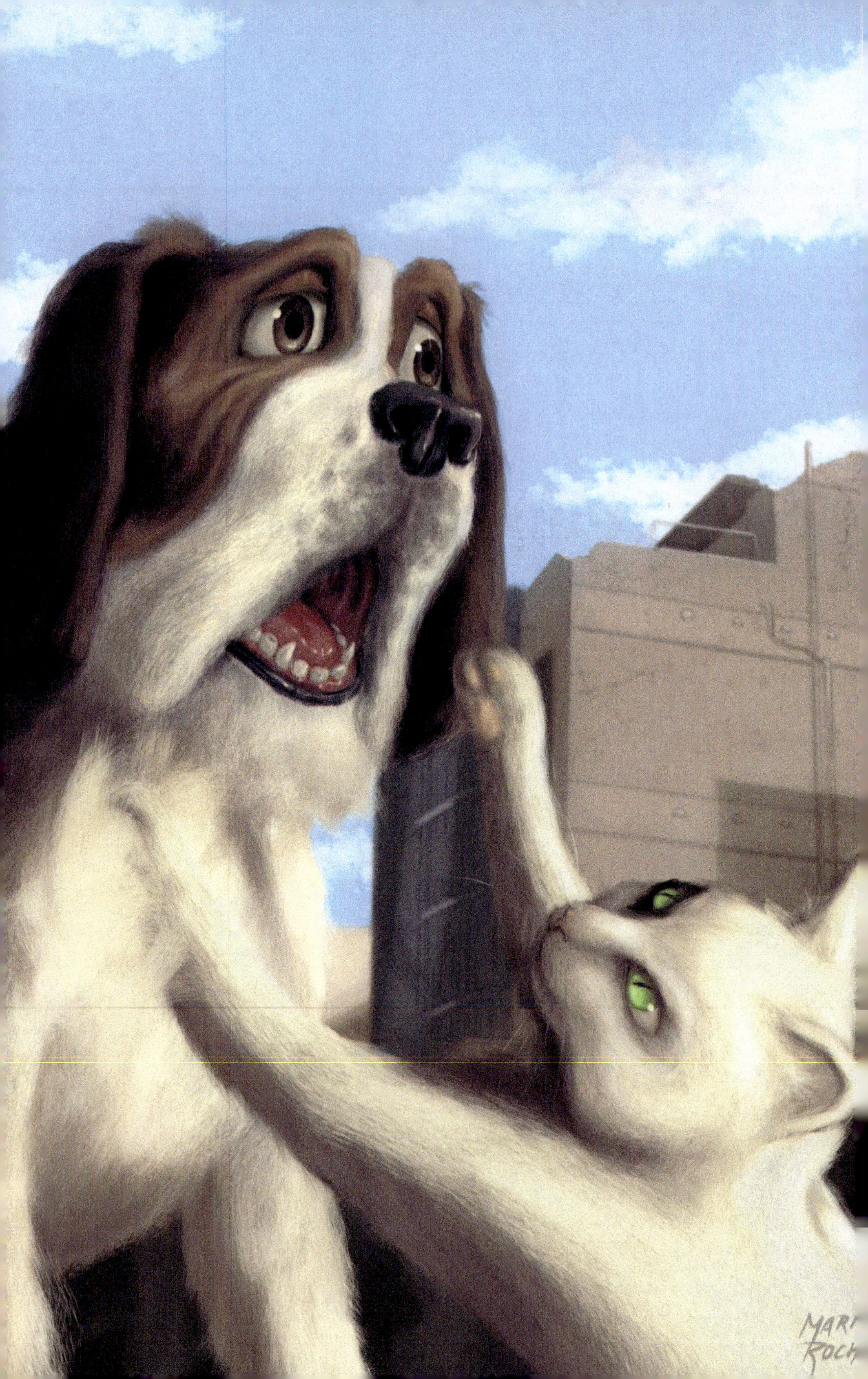

A sharp, muffled scream woke me up—it was the girl, staring out of the truck.

—Rex! —I called—. Wake up, sleepyhead, something's happening out there!

The big dog woke with a snort. We peeked through the trailer door and, to our horror, saw the red-eyed monster outside.

It had followed us!

Now that it was daylight, I could see it more clearly: its face was horrendous, as if it had melted. Its mouth was huge and red, with sharp fangs sticking out. But it wasn't an animal, because it walked like a person. It wore a torn, filthy black suit.

However, what struck me the most was how familiar that creature looked.

—By the love of my masters! —Rex trembled—. We have to get out of here!

We escaped through the truck's cab and ran until we were exhausted. When we finally looked back, the creature was gone.

—That monster is following us. It wants to kill me, I know it! —Rex whimpered.

—Why do you say that?

—Because… this isn't the first time I've seen it.

—We saw it two nights ago, remember?

—But I saw it before that —Rex admitted—. It's been following me for a while. It scares me, but if it tries to hurt the girl, or Kit-Ten, or you, Watson, I swear I'll kill it!

I kept thinking about that. It couldn't be a coincidence that it was following Rex. And that face… it was so familiar.

—Rex, I don't know if we can take care of the girl. What if zombies attack her? Or those bad humans in the green truck come back?

—I'll protect her. No matter what.

—And Kit-Ten?

—I'll protect him too —Rex said with determination.

—Rex, you can't protect them both at the same time. They'll kill you!

—Don't worry, I'll handle it all.

The sun rose higher, and we got thirsty. We drank from a stream, and Rex caught a fish, which he offered to the girl. But she refused.

—Humans only eat cooked food, remember? —I reminded him.

—I'd give anything to have hands and make a fire, —Rex lamented.

—If we can't give her food, she'll die, —I said, immediately regretting it after seeing the sadness on his face.

However, we soon realized we didn't need to worry. The girl wandered off into a small grove and came back with an orange. She cracked it open with a stone and ate it, smiling at us with her teeth stained orange.

—Wow, she's not as helpless as I thought, —I marveled.

—We could go to a store, —Rex suggested—. I saw a few along the way. Maybe there's still food for her.

It seemed like a good idea. We veered off the road and approached a huge building with faded letters that read:

W LMA T

The place was enormous, and a bad feeling churned in my gut. But Rex insisted, so we went in.

The building smelled like old, rotten food. We checked the shelves—there were only glasses, books, and kitchen appliances left.

—There's got to be something over there, —Rex insisted.

—Dog, I think we should leave. There's something here I don't like…

—Isn't that a can of food up there?

I followed his gaze. Sure enough, on one of the highest shelves, there was a can with a picture of a fish on it.

—I'll climb up, —I offered.

With two jumps, I was at the top. I pushed the can with my nose, and it clattered to the floor.

—Yes! —Rex cheered—. Now we've got food for the pup!

—I think with that…

I didn't get to finish.

Something big rushed toward the girl.

It was a zombie. One of the biggest I'd ever seen. He wore a bloody white apron and held a butcher's cleaver in his hand. His mouth buzzed with an annoying sound as drool dripped from his lips.

—Rex, watch out!

But it was too late.

The zombie grabbed the girl and, with rotten, saliva-covered teeth, sank his jaws into her arm.

CHAPTER 23

THE ATTACK

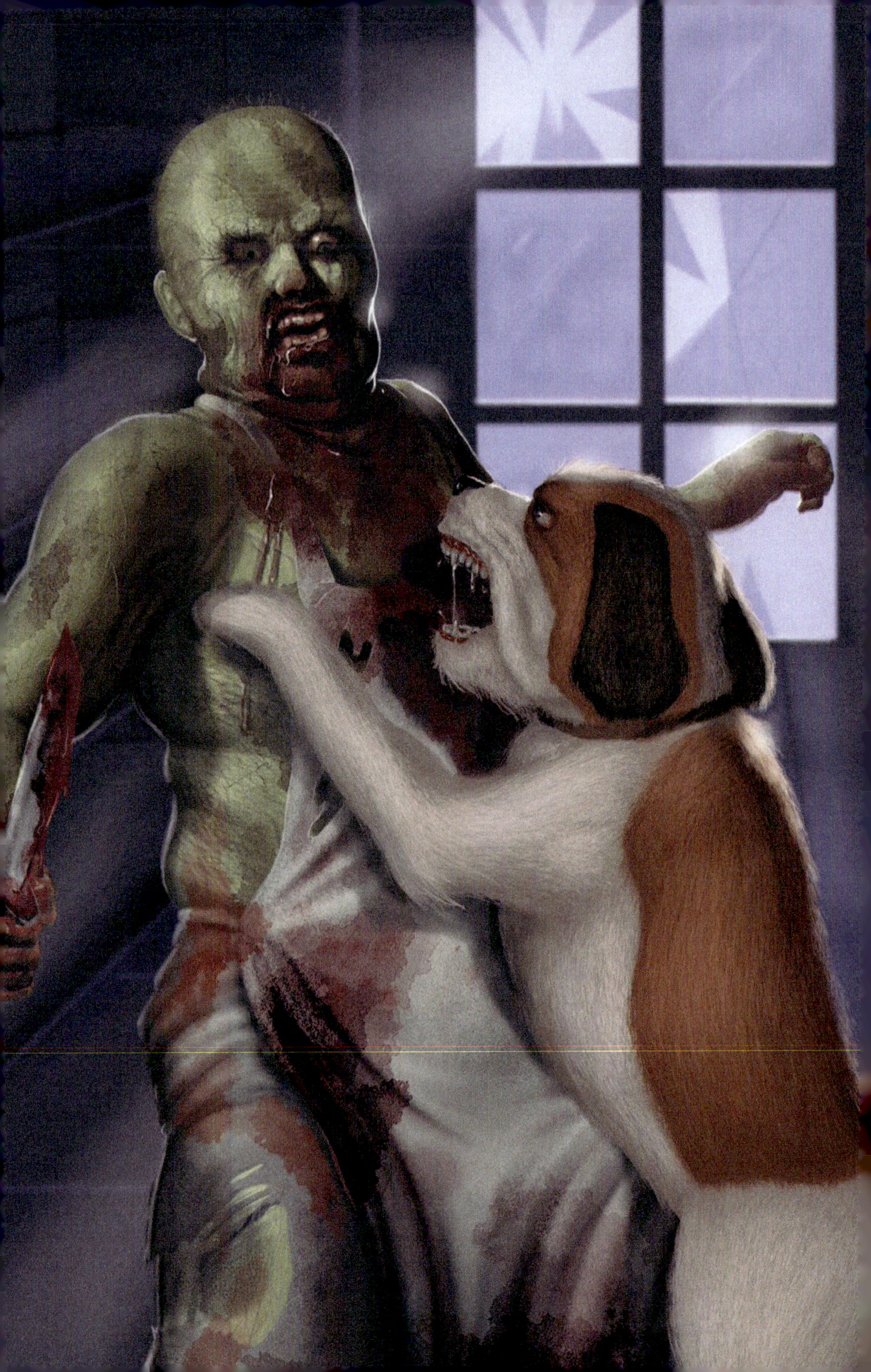

If you ask me, it was one of the slowest, most torturous moments of my life.

The zombie was as big as a wild boar—or maybe like the gorilla that had attacked us at the zoo. It grabbed the girl by the arm and sank its teeth into her flesh. She made muffled sounds and tried to pull away, but it was impossible.

Without thinking, I threw myself at the dead thing. It was pure instinct. I landed on its head and clawed at it furiously, but the zombie grabbed me by the tail and flung me across the room like a bag of potato chips.

Rex roared and attacked, slamming the zombie to the floor. He was a beast now, a terrifying force of nature. His paws tore into the creature's body, and his powerful jaws locked onto its neck, shaking it from side to side. In that moment, he wasn't good ol' Rex anymore—he was a predator you wouldn't dare approach.

The zombie finally went still, but even then, Rex kept biting and growling under his breath. The girl clutched her arm and sobbed quietly. Kit-Ten had fallen off Rex's back and was now hiding under a nearby shelf, trembling.

A few moments later, it was over. Rex moved away from the corpse and collapsed on the floor, his sides heaving, utterly exhausted.

—Rex, are you okay? —I asked, cautiously approaching.

—Yeah… but the zombie bit the girl.

—It doesn't look that bad —I assured him, inspecting the wound—. It's just a bite. I think she'll heal.

—I should've protected her better!

—Rex, it's not your fault! You're not some kind of super-dog.

Rex got back up, glancing at the motionless zombie lying in a pool of blood. He walked over to the girl and gently licked her arm. She stopped crying at the touch of his tongue.

—Come on, let's get out of here, —I suggested.

In silence, we left the supermarket.

Kit-Ten whimpered pitifully on Rex's back, and the girl tied a piece of her nightgown around her arm to bandage the wound.

—This girl is really smart! Her parents must have taught her a lot! —Rex said, cheering up a little.

We kept walking. Only later did I remember something that filled me with regret: in our rush to flee, we'd forgotten the can of food.

—It's too risky to go back now —I told Rex—. We'll find something else later.

We followed the road lined with abandoned cars, always keeping an eye out for zombies. Luckily, there weren't many, and the few we saw, we avoided by cutting through the tall grass.

By evening, the girl started to pale. Her breathing grew heavy, and when she removed the bandage, I saw something that filled me with dread: the wound was red and swollen, dotted with small white spots.

—Rex, the bite is worse than I thought.

The dog tried to lead her to a stream to drink water, but she shook her head and kept walking.

—We should keep moving —I told him—. There are too many dead around here. If they see us, she's done for.

—What's happening to her? Tell me, Watson! You know about medicine, don't you?

—I wish I did —I admitted, shaking my head—. I think the bite infected her… maybe she'll turn into one of them.

—No! —Rex howled—. We can't let that happen!
—I'm sorry, Big Guy. I don't have any answers.
The girl staggered, then collapsed onto the asphalt.
—Help me get her on my back! —Rex said, frantic.
—She's too heavy for you!
—I can do it! Please, help me!

We managed to lift the girl onto his back. Kit-Ten clung to his tail, and we kept moving until nightfall. By then, we had put enough distance between us and the zombies to feel a bit safer. We found an abandoned warehouse and laid the girl down on some bags of seeds. Exhausted, Rex flopped onto the floor.

—Are you okay? —I asked.
—Just… need to rest for a little while.

He looked terrible. The girl barely moved, breathing heavily in her feverish sleep. Next to her, Kit-Ten curled up and dozed off, blissfully oblivious to everything.

The wind picked up outside, and soon it started to rain. The raindrops hammered against the metal roof, accompanied by distant thunder.

I stayed awake all night, thinking about everything that had happened and what lay ahead. Our future felt dark, uncertain, and incredibly complicated.

I approached the girl: she was burning up with fever. Next to her, Rex's breathing was slow and labored.

I was nodding off near dawn when a chill ran down my spine. Something was wrong. I sensed a presence behind me—a hunch only a cat can feel.

I spun around, claws out and back arched.
Then I saw it.

It stood at the barn door, dripping with rainwater. Its tiger-like fangs gleamed in the dim light, and its long black claws tapped against the doorframe.

The red-eyed monster had found us again.

It stepped forward, its horrible face twisted into a gruesome grin.

—Rex! —I meowed in terror—. Rex, wake up! The monster is back!

But Rex, too exhausted to move, kept sleeping.

CHAPTER 24

THE MONSTER RETURNS

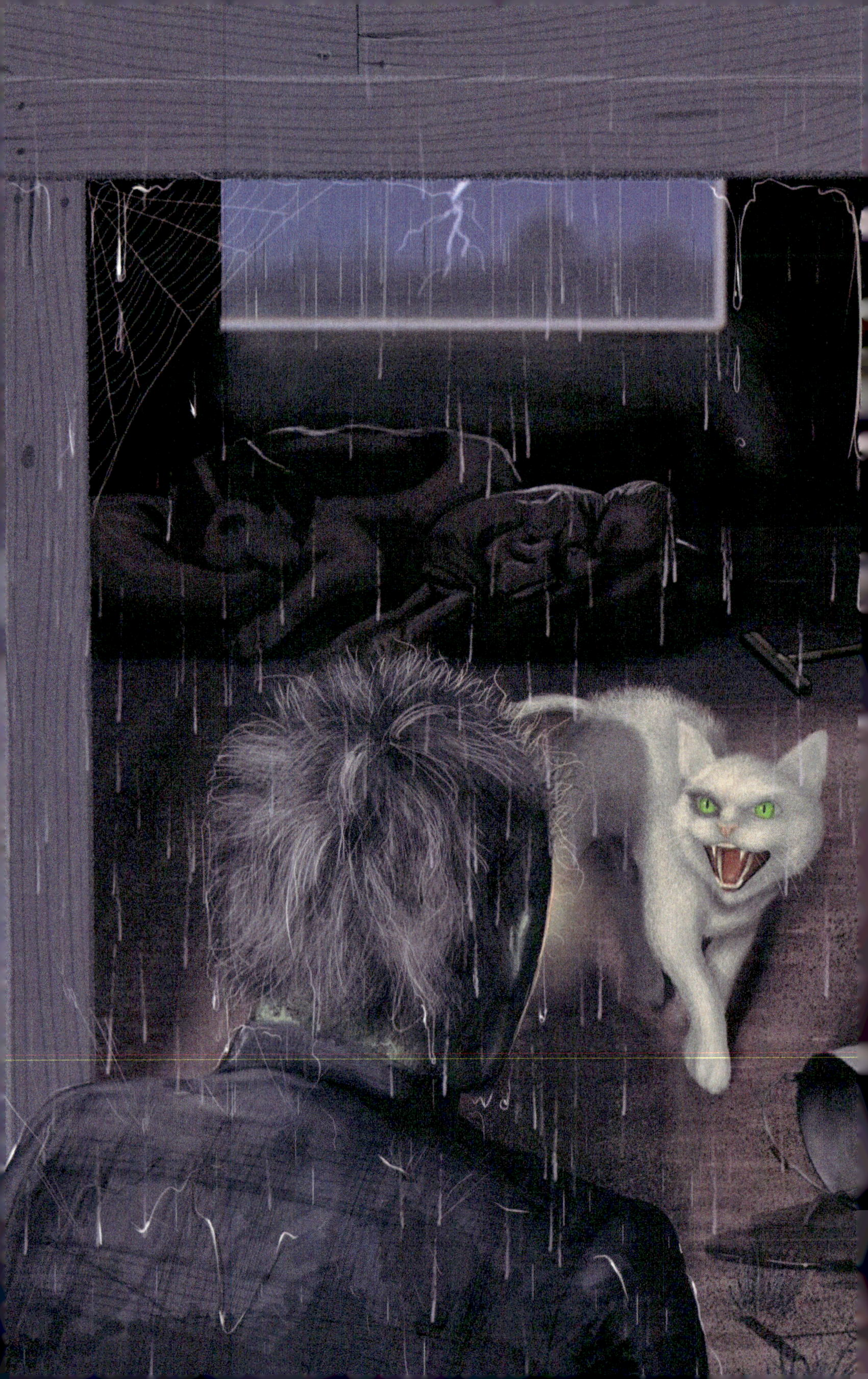

The storm outside worsened. The trees shook, and the thunder made the ground tremble. The red-eyed monster took another step forward. I clawed at Rex, but the damn mutt wouldn't wake up. The monster moved even closer.

There was something about it... something terrifyingly familiar.

I stepped between the monster and my friends. I knew I couldn't stop it, but maybe I could delay it.

—Rex, damn it, wake up already! —I meowed with all my strength.

The thing advanced again. I lunged forward and clawed at its body. The monster tried to grab me, but I dodged, meowing like crazy. Despite my attacks, it kept coming. Just a few steps separated it from Rex and the girl.

Desperate, I leapt onto its face, but this time, the creature smacked me on the head, leaving me dazed. I hit the floor hard.

Its movements grew quicker and more erratic. I followed its gaze and realized why: it had just seen the girl. It was a walking corpse, after all. But why did it have such a horrible face?

The thing rushed toward the sleeping girl, and that's when Rex finally woke up. With his huge head, he rammed the monster, knocking it back.

And in that exact moment... it hit me.

I remembered where I'd seen that monster before.

It was so obvious I cursed myself for not recalling it sooner. I got up with effort and stood beside Rex, who was growling, his neck fur bristling.

—Rex, listen...

—Not now, Watson. I have to kill this thing, or it'll hurt the girl!

—Rex, you said your master was at a party when the zombie invasion happened. Do you remember what kind of party it was?

—Well... no, —the dog said, still growling.

—Were people wearing costumes?

—I don't know, Watson! Get out of the way, I'm going to finish this thing!

—Rex, I think the monster is your master.

The dog froze. He looked at me with wide eyes.

—What did you say?

—That monster... I think it's your master. Look!

Without another word, I ran toward the zombie and jumped onto its face.

Only it wasn't a real face—it was a mask. A vampire mask.

That's why it seemed familiar! I'd seen that face in dozens of horror movies.

With little effort, I ripped off the mask, whose eyes were two red lights powered by batteries. Beneath it, a dead human face was revealed, and Rex recognized it immediately.

—No! —Rex whimpered, his voice full of grief—. It's not true!

—I'm sorry, Dog. Your human was at a costume party when the invasion happened. He must have been bitten by a zombie and transformed into this, still wearing the mask and costume. You couldn't recognize him because you refused to use your nose. Plus, the smell of dead humans changes. And remember what the turtle said? Many zombies try to return to their previous lives. Your human must have seen you and followed you everywhere. But now he's dangerous. He's seen the girl, and he'll attack her any second now. We have to stop him!

—No, no, no! —Rex cried—. My master is waiting for me in the land of healthy humans! He's not a zombie! He's not dead!

—Rex, please! You have to stop him, or...

At that moment, the zombie dressed as Dracula got back up. He glanced at me with disinterest, then at Rex. For a brief moment, his dead eyes seemed to recognize him.

But then, his gaze shifted to the girl. His face twisted into savage rage—the same expression I'd seen on other zombies before they attacked humans.

—Rex, you have to stop him!

—I won't attack my own master, —the dog said, tears streaming down his face—. I can't. I can't...

CHAPTER 25

THE GODDESS OF ALL CATS

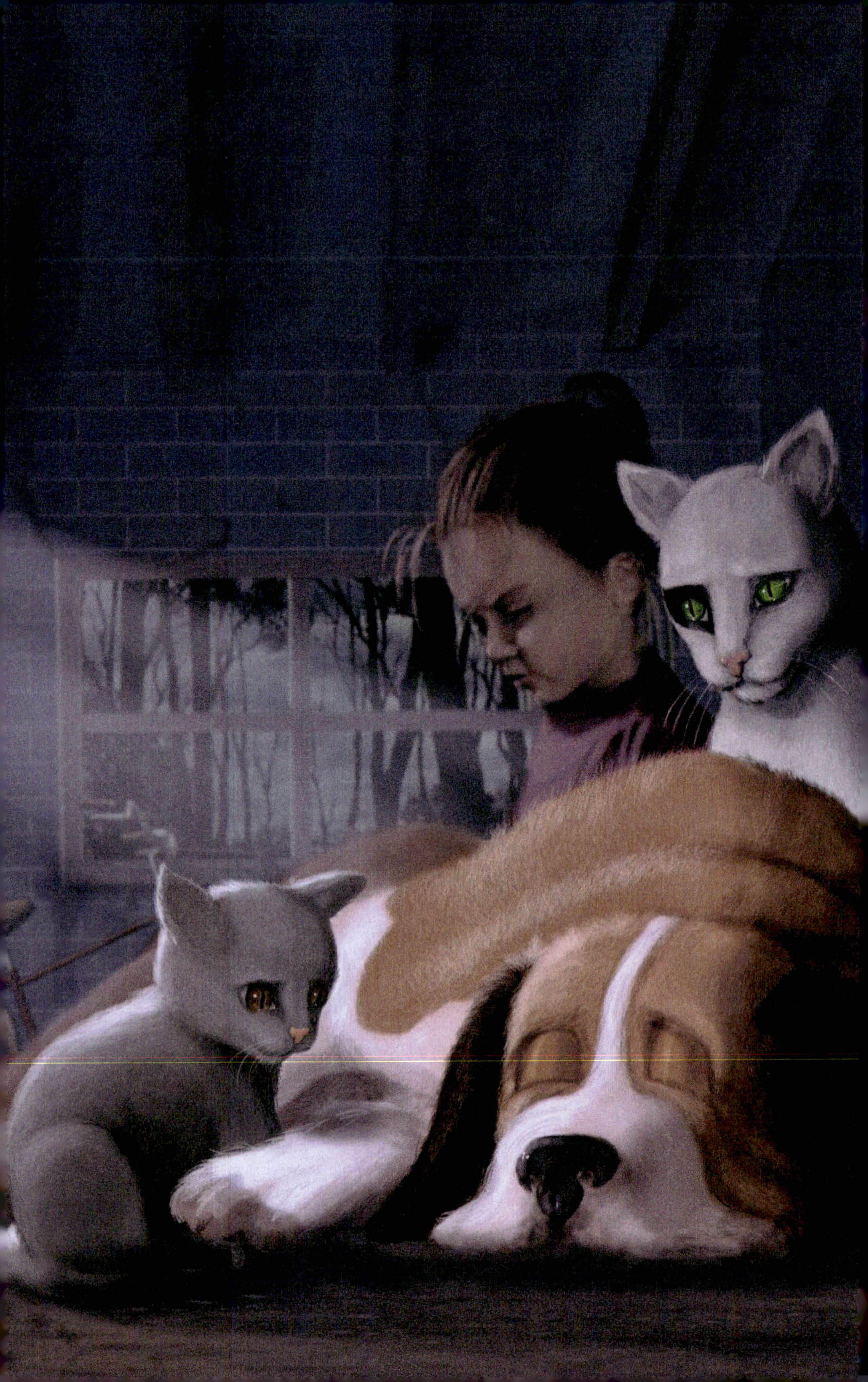

The zombie dressed as Dracula advanced, passing by Rex, who whimpered and shrank back. The zombie leaned down to bite the girl, and that's when I attacked with all my strength.

I clung to his head with my teeth, claws, and back paws, determined to hurt him. The monster, enraged by my interference, grabbed me by the tail. I thought it was the end when he grabbed my neck with both hands, ready to snap it like a twig.

And that's when Rex, good old heartbroken Rex, sprang into action.

He knocked the zombie down with a single shove and went for its neck. The struggle was intense but brief. After a few moments, the zombie let out a screech, its legs stiffened, and it went still.

Rex turned toward me, his eyes filled with tears.

—I swear… I swear I didn't want to do it…

—I know, Rex. But you did the right thing. That thing wasn't your master anymore.

The dog didn't seem to hear me. He lay down next to the girl. I approached and asked if he was okay, but the Saint Bernard didn't respond.

Outside, the storm eased a little, but the wind still howled through the holes in the barn's roof. It was still far from dawn, but you could already sense it would be one of those days when the rain falls incessantly, and the fields, buildings, and air fill with a silvery, misty gray.

—Rex, are you okay? —I insisted—. You didn't do anything wrong. Things have changed. That's all.

But the dog didn't say a word; he just lay there with his eyes half-closed and wet.

The night dragged on slowly.

At times, the girl got worse and seemed on the verge of death. Rex sank into a state of unconsciousness I couldn't pull him out of, not even by licking his face. I sat by the group, waiting for something to happen, though I didn't know what.

And what happened was that dawn came, and everything remained the same. The sun was hidden behind clouds. It kept raining. Water dripped through the roof in large drops. A cold wind blew in through the barn's open door.

Later, Kit-Ten woke up hungry. The only thing I could offer him was a cockroach I found while moving some planks. Still, the kitten seemed pleased, rubbing against my back after eating.

Neither Rex nor the girl stirred.

Time passed, afternoon faded, and I started fearing the worst. The dog was breathing very slowly. The girl, on the other hand, seemed to be running, though she lay still. She burned with fever.

—Mrs. Bast, goddess of all cats, if you're there, please do something for the dog —I prayed out loud, something I'd never done before in my life—. Don't let... don't let him go. I won't manage Kit-Ten, nor the girl. And, above all, I don't want to lose him... —I looked at his brown and white fur, his floppy ears falling over his snout, and licked him a little—. Because this damn dog has become my friend. Amen.

At dawn the next day, something unexpected happened: the girl opened her eyes and stood up. She was completely healed; she hadn't turned into a zombie. Apparently, she was immune to the virus.

The little human looked at me and smiled, then petted Kit-Ten (who seemed very happy to see her awake again), and then crouched in front of the dog. She frowned and looked at me. At that moment, I wished I could explain what had happened, but I didn't know how.

Still, the girl seemed to figure it out because she saw the zombie still lying in a corner of the barn.

The rain had stopped. The girl went outside and returned with a container full of water. She tried to give Rex a drink, but he didn't react.

She went out again and came back with some strong-smelling herbs. She passed them under the dog's nose: nothing.

For the next two days, we stayed like that: the girl going back and forth, trying different herbal remedies for the dog, always with no results. There was a stream nearby, and I caught some fish. The girl only ate fruits and herbs she collected from the forest. There was no improvement in Rex; he seemed to have decided to die of sadness.

—Come on, dog, wake up already —I told him one night when we felt very sad and alone—. Please. The world's already too messed up to lose friends.

The girl and even Kit-Ten were crying. I lay down on the big dog's back and slept there. The other two also curled up around the big dog, as if trying to protect him with the warmth of their bodies. And that's how we spent the night, thinking it would be the last time we'd see Rex alive.

The next day, I was awakened by a few licks on my face. I opened my eyes: it was the dog, who had finally woken up.

—Good morning, dear friend —Rex said with his goofy, tender smile.

And I pounced on his neck and hugged him like I never thought I'd hug a dog.

CHAPTER 26

TOWARDS THE END OF THE WORLD

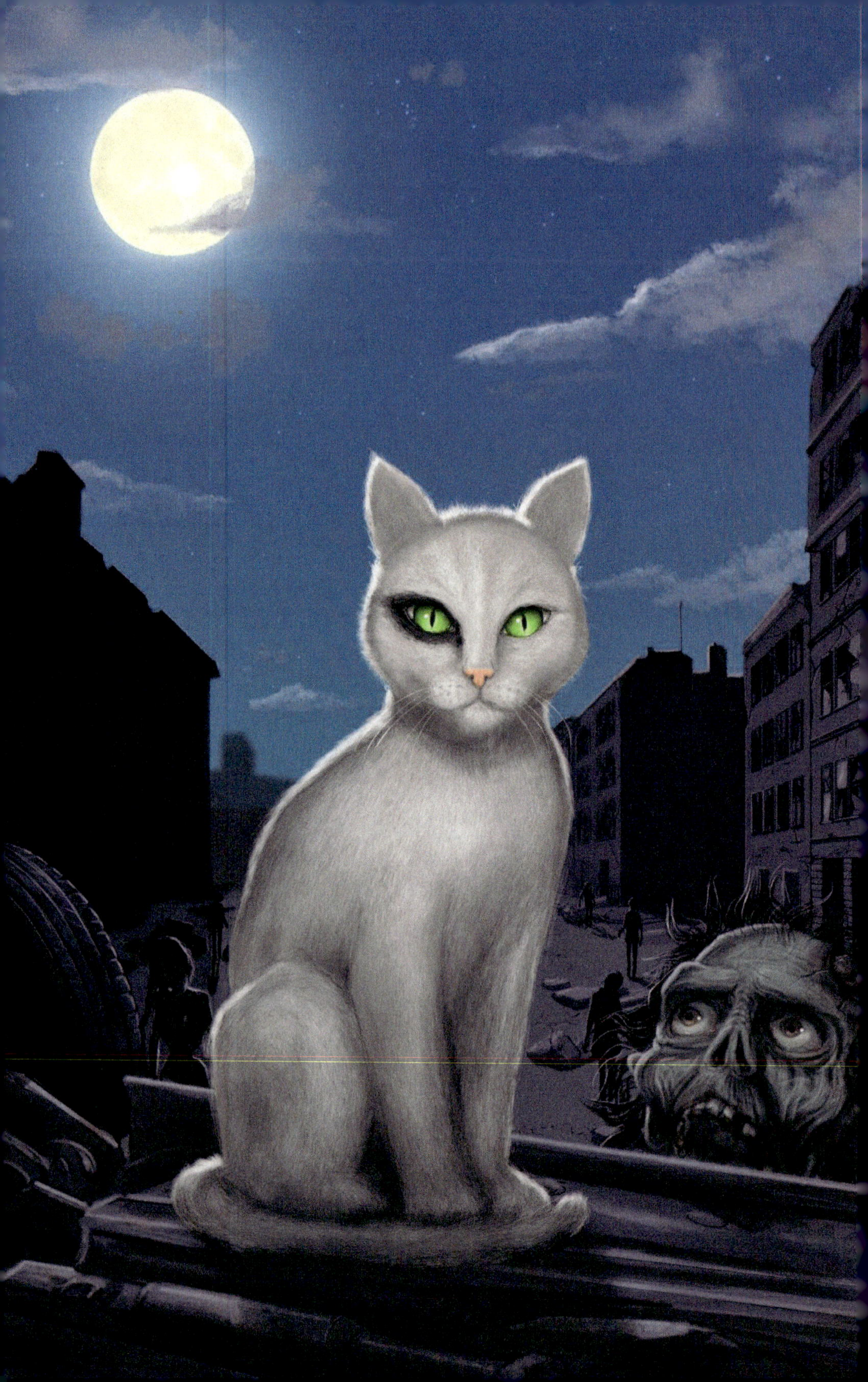

Rex had lost a lot of weight and was very weak; yet, the first thing he did was dig a grave for what had once been his master. We helped as much as we could—me with my claws, the girl with her hands, and Kit-Ten scraping at the dirt with his tiny, sharp nails.

Then, Rex dragged the body into the hole and stood silently, his eyes filled with sorrow.

—Goodbye, my dear master. We shared great moments together, and I will never forget you —he said, shedding tears of sadness.

We covered the body with earth, the sound of falling dirt echoing in the quiet morning. No prayers, no speeches—just the whispering wind, and the weight of what had been left unsaid.

We left the grave behind and continued our journey. For the first time in what felt like ages, the sun warmed our backs. Its light seemed almost too bright for a world so battered and broken.

—You know, maybe that human refuge doesn't even exist after all, and it's just an illusion —said Rex, suddenly in a good mood, sniffing the air—. But at least we have to try. We have nothing to lose, do we?

Before I could answer, a blue-winged butterfly drifted down from nowhere and landed on Rex's nose. The dog went cross-eyed, trying to look at it. We all burst out laughing—Kit-Ten, the girl, even me.

At first, Rex didn't understand why we were laughing, but soon he rolled over on the grass, letting out big, goofy chuckles. The butterfly floated away, disappearing into the pale blue sky, and we never saw it again.

—What were you going to say? —Rex asked, once our laughter faded.

—Me?

—Yes. I said maybe the human refuge didn't exist, and you were about to say something before the butterfly interrupted us.

—Oh, well... I forgot.

But that was a lie.

Because I knew exactly what I was going to say.

That the refuge didn't matter all that much anymore.

Because we had already found what we were searching for. Rex had been looking for someone to guide him, and he had found me—a reluctant leader, but a leader nonetheless.

I had been looking for safety, for someone to take care of me, and I had found Rex.

Kit-Ten was searching for a family, and he had found us.

And the girl, well, she had lost everything and stumbled into our strange, fragile world. What she needed was someone to protect her, someone to walk beside her, and that's what we were.

We had found each other in the ruins of a collapsing world, and that was something rare and precious.

But of course, I didn't tell Rex any of that. We cats hide our emotions; we bury them deep, like treasures under the sand. We prefer to seem aloof, detached, untouched by sentiment.

But we love.

Oh, how we love.

We love in the quiet moments when the wind smells of rain and the grass bends beneath our paws. We love the warmth of sunlight on our fur, the sound of leaves rustling overhead. We love sleeping in boxes, climbing rooftops to watch the stars, and curling up next to those we care about.

Above all, we love waking up and finding that those we love are still close. Even in a world falling apart, even when fear looms large, that love is a light that never goes out.

Rex, meanwhile, looked at me as if somehow he could read my thoughts.

—What are you thinking about, dear Cat? —he asked with a smile.

—Nothing, dear Dog —I replied, masking my thoughts—. Nothing at all.

And so we walked on, beneath a clear blue sky, toward a destination no one—not even the great goddess Bast—could ever know.

But for the first time in a long while, I wasn't afraid of what lay ahead.

aaa

AUTHOR'S NOTE AND DEDICATION

I dedicate this book to my son, Leandro Croche, a devoted fan of Watson, and, of course, to all the pets that have left their paw prints on my life:

Bobi, a stray dog who taught me to walk when I was just one year old.

Collie, a mutt who hated baths and ran away the moment he heard the word *water*.

Surubí, an Angora cat with fur as wild as the fish he was named after.

Mencho, a mischievous dog who destroyed all of my mother's plants.

Pirata, an old one-eyed cat who, in a way, inspired the character of Watson.

Pinky, Mencho's mother and the fierce protector of our home.

Morena, a Great Dane who turned our garden into a battlefield of holes for five years.

Pepa, a Patagonian conure with a soft spot for bread soaked in milk.

Bomba, a black cat who brought us nothing but good luck—as all black cats do.

And to my current companions:

Boni, a ten-year-old little dog with a heart bigger than her size.

Teniente Sally, a five-year-old cat with a commanding presence.

Van Helsing, an eighty-four—or maybe eighty-five—year-old tortoise who has been by my side since childhood.

Pets make us happy. They complete us. They make us better human beings.

Let's cherish them, protect them, and be grateful for the love they give, because as Watson himself says:

"The world is already too cruel to go through it without friends."

Printed in Great Britain
by Amazon